"Jack? Kelly?"

Frantic, she ran into the living room. There was no sign of Jack and Kelly.

Slowly, Hayley moved into the room. Following a crepe paper streamer, she found the end clutched tightly in Kelly's bloodied hand. Jack was slumped against the wall behind her. Blood had dried around a perfect hole in the middle of his forehead.

Hayley opened her mouth to scream, but a hand that smelled strongly of scotch clamped over it. She recognized Bruce Donner's voice as it rasped in her ear. Breaking free, Hayley ran screaming from the apartment.

Her elderly downstairs neighbors threw open their door at her frantic pounding, nearly jumping out of the way as she stumbled into their apartment.

"He killed them," Hayley wailed, shaking like a leaf. "He killed Jack and Kelly!"

Footsteps thumped down the staircase outside the apartment door. Hayley saw Bruce race into the street. He had to be looking for her.

"Stop him!" she shouted. "He's getting away!"

Other Books By Clare McNally

Somebody Come And Play
There He Keeps Them Very Well

STAGE FRIGHT

Clare McNally

TOR®

A TOM DOHERTY ASSOCIATES BOOK
NEW YORK

STAGE FRIGHT

Cover art by Paul E. Stinson

A Tor book
Published by Tom Doherty Associates, Inc.
175 Fifth Avenue
New York, N.Y. 10010

Tor® is a registered trademark of Tom Doherty Associates, Inc.

ISBN: 0-812-54839-6

First edition: August 1995

Printed in the United States of America

0 9 8 7 6 5 4 3 2 1

THIS BOOK IS DEDICATED WITH LOVE
TO THE MEMORY
OF MY BROTHER,
MICHAEL McNALLY,
WHO MADE ME LAUGH A LOT

SPECIAL THANKS TO
SUSAN GEISBUSCH WALMSELY

I HOPE OUR FRIENDSHIP NEVER BECOMES
A "CLOAK AND DAGGER" MYSTERY!

Prologue

Y ou're a brilliant young woman, my dear."

Hayley Seagel turned toward the rich, deep baritone voice and smiled as she tried to identify the gray-haired man who had spoken. A critic from one of the local tv stations, she thought, but what was his name? She made a quick mental check of the guest list but came up blank.

The man took Hayley's hand in his and smiled back.

"One thousand performances," he said. " 'By Blood or by Marriage' has certainly come a long way since its opening night at the Bluebay Theater. And as a director, so have you."

Hayley winced. "You saw that performance? So many things went wrong!"

"But even so," the man said, "I could tell it was destined for success. I saw it again when Annie Hammond played the role of Bianca. She was perfect for the part."

"We were sorry to see her go," Hayley said, remembering the glamorous, but hard-working, soap opera star, "but she had too many other obligations. I think Kelly Palmer makes a wonderful Bianca."

"Not old enough," the critic said bluntly. "Still, she was impressive. The whole cast is impressive. You ought to move the show to Broadway. *By Blood or by Marriage* is a triumph."

A woman with a snow-white bouffant edged up to them.

"A wonderful mystery!" Grace Winchell said. "After all the reviews I've read over the past three years, I wonder why it took me so long to see the show. You had me guessing right up to the end."

Hayley did recognize Grace, a syndicated gossip columnist.

"Thank you," she said. "Of course, I had a lot of help from Bruce."

Grace frowned. "Bruce?"

"She means Bruce Donner," the gray-haired man explained. He cleared his throat. "Let's give credit where it's really due, shall we? I find it hard to believe Donner had much to do with the play's success."

Hayley lost her smile.

"He's the writer," she said. "He had everything to do with this. You know he won a Tony a few years back, don't you?"

"And now he seems to be resting on his laurels," Grace replied. "Short of getting drunk and making a spectacle of himself at social gatherings, what has he done lately?"

The reviewer put a firm hand on Hayley's shoulder. She tried to be graceful, resisting the urge to shake it off.

"If it wasn't for Bruce Donner," she said firmly, "I

wouldn't have this company. He's my mentor and friend."

"What I mean to say," the older man told her, "is that talk throughout the theatrical microcosm of Boston is that your association with Bruce Donner will eventually bring you down."

Hayley was ready to defend Bruce, to say she would never turn against the man who had given her both financial and emotional support ever since her little theatrical company had begun. But the guests had turned away and were staring disapprovingly at Bruce, who stood by the bar. He seemed to sense he was being watched, because he turned toward Hayley, smiling and waving. The action put him off balance and he stumbled a little. He grabbed the edge of the bar for support. Grace snickered. The tv critic shook his head slightly.

Before Hayley could say a word, someone caught the crook of her elbow and steered her away from the two.

"Watch out," Jack Langley said teasingly. "Hayley Seagel's got that glint in her eyes."

"Oh, did you hear what they said?" Hayley asked, her shoulders hunched up like an angry bird's. "What a pair of snobs. I bet those two couldn't write a three-line poem. Bruce Donner is brilliant."

Jack grabbed a pair of full champagne glasses from a passing tray.

"Bruce *was* brilliant," he corrected her. "A Tony award eight years ago doesn't carry much clout today. Especially for someone who drank away the last five years."

"Bruce has problems," Hayley admitted. "I don't think he's gotten over losing his parents in that horrible boating accident. I know there's another play in him, and I refuse to give up on an old schoolmate,"—she lowered her voice— "the way everyone else seems to have done."

Jack gently caressed Hayley's round cheek as he looked into her eyes.

"You're the sweetest thing," he said. "You have the most caring heart."

He kissed her, then toyed with the pearl and opal necklace she wore.

"It looks nice with that dress," he said.

Hayley stepped back and turned this way and that to show off the necklace. The opals seemed to pick up color from the pale green moire satin of her off-the-shoulder gown, while the pearls caught the light in the same way as the teardrop beads covering the dress's bodice.

"It's beautiful," she said. "I was so surprised to find it on my desk after the show."

"A gift for one thousand performances," Jack said, "and for our first anniversary as a couple."

Hayley smiled. "But our official anniversary isn't until the day after tomorrow."

Jack kissed her again. "Then I'll have to give you another gift the day after tomorrow."

Hayley felt intoxicated with joy. Jack had had that effect on Hayley from the moment he'd been introduced to her by Dinah Elburn, the company's publicist and Hayley's good friend. Maybe it was the way his blue eyes squinted when he smiled, maybe it was the warm, almost protective way he touched her . . .

"Can we interrupt you lovebirds long enough to say congratulations?" Dinah's voice cut into her thoughts as the woman appeared at Hayley's side, Bruce a step behind her. Dinah looked almost ethereal, with her white hair and light blue eyes. She wore a white linen suit shot through with silver threads and silver jewelry that looked heavy enough to bend her slender neck. She gave Hayley a warm hug, then pulled Bruce forward. Hayley felt Jack tense in his presence. She squeezed Jack's hand as she smiled at her partners.

Bruce hugged the breath out of her, then planted a kiss that left the aroma of scotch on her cheek.

"She's remarkable, isn't she?" Bruce asked loudly, keeping one arm tightly around Hayley's shoulders. "I just heard Abner Gallo talking about a move to New York City."

Abner Gallo. *That* was the name of the tv critic.

"He said the same thing to me," Hayley said coolly. Gallo's comments about Bruce had tainted everything else he had said, as far as she was concerned.

"Oh, I'm not surprised at that," Dinah drawled. "I knew 'By Blood or by Marriage' was New York material from the moment I read it. Bruce has so much talent."

Bruce nuzzled Dinah's cheek, mumbling something Hayley could not make out despite their closeness.

Dinah was beaming, even though Bruce was too drunk to really know what he was doing. Hayley supposed any flirting from a younger man—and Bruce was at least ten years younger than Dinah—was welcome to the older woman. Hayley guessed that in her heart, Dinah was ten years younger than Bruce.

"I got my start here in Boston, you know," Bruce said, stepping away from Hayley and slinging an arm around Dinah's shoulder. " 'Course, I don't plan to be up here forever. Broadway's my real home. As soon as I finish my new play, I'm heading for the Great White Way."

A heavyset young man with a round face and bright blue eyes joined the group. "I'd love to see your new work, Mr. Donner," he said. "I was only thirteen when you won the Tony for 'Red Herring.' I read the play, and I thought it was just terrific."

Hayley smiled at Roger Moran, who was the youngest member of her company.

"I think Roger's your biggest fan," she said indulgently.

Bruce lifted his glass to the young man.

"Obviously a person of good taste," he said, as he hugged Hayley once again, "like you. Now, when I leave, I'll have two people to come with me."

"Two?" Jack asked.

"Dinah's coming to New York, aren't you, Dinah?"

"You bet," Dinah said, but Hayley sensed she was only humoring the man.

"And Hayley has to come," Bruce went on. "A remarkable person like Hayley should be working on Broadway. I don't know what I'd do without her."

Hayley tried to smile, to accept Bruce's words as simple flattery, but she couldn't. She never felt comfortable when Bruce flirted with her, especially when he was drunk.

"Hayley, I think Kelly is flagging you down," Jack interrupted, mentioning another of the performers in Hayley's company.

Hayley looked beyond the sea of guests to the hors d'oeuvres table, where Kelly stood, filling a plate. She frowned slightly at Jack; Kelly hadn't called her at all. Then she realized that Jack was giving her a graceful way to move on. She smiled at her lover, grateful for his tact.

"Excuse me," she said, breaking away from Bruce's strong arm.

Kelly was stuffing a piece of sashimi into her mouth when Hayley caught up with her. Hayley considered the pretty young woman the sister she had never had. They even looked alike, with the same strawberry blond hair and green eyes.

"Jack said you were waving to me," Hayley said, reaching for a plate.

"I wasn't," Kelly said, puzzled.

"I know you weren't," Hayley said with a smile. "Jack was rescuing me from Bruce's clutches." Kelly laughed ruefully.

"I think that guy has the hots for you, in case you didn't notice."

"Oh, Kelly, that's ridiculous," Hayley said. "We've been friends for years. It's nothing more than that."

Kelly glanced across the room at Bruce, who was carrying on an animated conversation with Roger.

"I don't think so," Kelly said. "I can tell these things. Bruce just seems to melt when you're near him."

Hayley thought for a moment, realizing that lately Bruce had been flirting with her more than usual. They'd always teased each other, but never once had Hayley thought Bruce was actually in love with her.

"I don't want to think about it," she said. "Bruce is my friend, and that's all."

"Try telling that to Bruce," Kelly said. "Ever since you took up with Jack, he's been depressed, and it's been worse lately, with you two wrapped up in your anniversary. He's talking more and more about Broadway, and his play—and he's drinking a lot more."

Hayley nodded. Kelly had put a voice to her own worries. "The accident that killed his parents happened around this time of year," she said. "Bruce always gets melancholy this time."

"It's worse than usual," Kelly said. "Maybe the fact that he hasn't been able to finish his play is compounding the problem."

"He will," Hayley said with confidence. "A talent like that can never die out completely."

She shifted from one foot to the other, looking around the party.

"Can we change the subject?" she asked. "This is supposed to be a happy occasion."

"Subject changed," Kelly said. She jabbed her fork into a pile of marinated mushrooms, tasted one, and made a rapturous face.

"Olive oil, garlic, and wine," she said. "Perfect. The food here is incredible, Hayley."

Hayley laughed at the deftness with which talk of Bruce was pushed aside. Kelly could brighten almost any situation. It was one of the reasons Hayley had taken to her when they'd first met, a few years earlier.

"Anyway, I haven't had a chance to say congratulations," Kelly said. "Can you believe we've been doing this for over three years?"

"It's been hard work, but fun." She looked directly at her friend. "You know I couldn't have done it without you, and Jack, and Bruce—and the rest of the cast, of course." She sighed. "I guess it's time for me to make a speech."

Kelly grabbed the plate from her hands and started filling it.

"Not until you've tasted some of this," she said, handing the hors d'oeuvres to Hayley.

Hayley laughed and allowed herself a few moments to enjoy the food. Then she called for everyone's attention. She gave a brief talk, full of thank-yous and congratulations. Her speech was frequently interrupted by loud applause, and all the party-goers gave the show's cast and crew a standing ovation as Hayley called them up to take a bow. Jack stood beside her, an arm around her waist. Dinah held her hand. It wasn't until the guests had broken into groups again that Hayley realized Bruce was no longer in the room.

But people kept stepping up to congratulate her, and Hayley became too caught up in the evening to think about her partner. Later, she and Jack went home and the two brought the perfect night to a perfect end.

The clock radio on Hayley's dresser clicked over to 7:00 A.M., and the voice of "Boston Bob" Baker filled her bedroom. Jack groaned, rolled across her, and slapped the radio to silence. Then he put his arms around Hayley and kissed her.

"Forgot to turn off the alarm," he said.

Hayley snuggled into his neck.

"Uh-huh," she said. "I have to get up. Dinah arranged an interview for me with the *Globe*. It's at eight-thirty."

"What kind of nut schedules an interview for 8:30 on a Sunday morning?" Jack wanted to know. "Doesn't that woman know Sunday's a day of rest?"

"It was the only time the reporter had free," Hayley said. "He's spending the weekend here, at his summer home; he's off to Chicago this afternoon, and won't be back for a week."

She gave Jack another kiss, then rolled out of bed. Jack threw himself across the bed and buried his head under Hayley's pillow. Hayley left the bathroom door open as she washed up, talking to Jack as if she had his full attention.

"Do you think I should wear my yellow dress?" she asked. "Or maybe the white knit suit with the gold trim? I've got that nice hat . . ."

"The yellow," Jack mumbled in reply.

"Or maybe the dark blue . . ."

Now Jack hoisted himself up on an elbow and squinted at her.

"What difference does it make?" he asked. "The pictures will all be in black-and-white."

Mouth dripping with toothpaste foam, Hayley made a face at him.

"Eight-thirty on a Sunday morning," Jack growled.

Hayley came out of the bathroom, rolling a curling iron into her hair.

"Who are you to talk about work hours?" she asked. "I've known you to stay at the lab until two or three in the morning!"

"Dedication," Jack said, lying back with his hands behind his head. "The mark of a great scientist."

"It's the mark of any good professional," Hayley replied.

She finished curling her hair, then went to her dresser and started pulling out lingerie. Jack rolled out of bed and came up behind her, hugging her tightly.

"Eight-thirty?" he whispered, nuzzling the back of her neck.

"Sorry, Jack," Hayley said. "Not enough time. I've got to grab a quick breakfast, then stop at the theater to pick up some notes."

"You're no fun," Jack moaned, heading for the bathroom.

"I'll make it up to you tonight," Hayley said to the closed door as she pulled on her slip. "How about veal marsala? With zabaglione for dessert?"

Jack said something unintelligible.

"What?"

Spitting sounds, running water, then: "Make it chocolate truffle cake, and you've got a deal."

Hayley laughed. "You drive a hard bargain, but okay."

By the time Jack emerged from the bathroom, Hayley was fully dressed. She reached for a pair of hoop earrings that were hooked over the ears of a little crystal mouse. There was a row of crystal animals on her dresser, all gifts from Jack. After one more embrace, they said goodbye.

Hayley lived on the upper floor of a two-family house

a short distance from downtown Boston. The street was filled with children playing and families on their way to church. Hayley waved hello to a familiar jogger who passed her house every morning, then got into her car and drove off.

If she'd left home just a few minutes later, she would have run into Bruce, staggering around the corner, cradling his head in one hand. Mewling with the pain of a deadly hangover, Bruce stopped to stare at Hayley's house. He knew Jack was there. He knew that the stuck-up computer nerd had spent the night with Hayley. Damn! Why had Dinah ever introduced them?

Hayley wasn't going to come to New York with him. She'd said as much last night. But if she wouldn't remain his partner, he'd make sure no one else could have her.

On Monday, Hayley had meetings with several potential backers for her next production. The tally, after hours of trying to prove herself and her company, came to one definite supporter, two maybes, and a fourth who decided that, good reputation or not, she needed more experience before he'd take the risk. Hayley was glad when the day came to an end. She hated negotiating. Her talents were in the production end of the business. But Bruce had called the previous night, claiming to be sick, and begging her to take on the interviews.

"Sick?" Jack had said as they enjoyed chocolate truffle cake at the Floating Dock. "More like a twenty-four-hour hangover."

"Be kind," Hayley replied.

"But tomorrow is our anniversary," Jack reminded. "I was hoping to spend the day together. You know, a bike ride along the Charles River, making love . . ."

Hayley smiled. "It sounds wonderful. But this is important. We can meet in the late afternoon, can't we?"

Jack had shrugged. "I suppose."

Now, driving home from the last interview, Hayley looked forward to spending the rest of the day with her beloved Jack. She thought over the year they'd had together, and all the wonderful times they'd had. Jack was an affectionate and caring person, even if he was more than a little impatient with weakness in others. He couldn't understand how a man could drink himself helpless the way Bruce had done.

As she passed Louisburg Square, she pushed thoughts of Bruce from her mind. Today was for her and Jack alone, at least, what was left of today. And there was always tonight . . .

She reached across the seat to touch the small package beside her. Sparkling holographic foil and curled ribbons of silver, blue and black concealed Jack's anniversary gift. Hayley had spent weeks trying to find the perfect wristwatch. It was gold and silver, simple yet bold in design, with the analog dial Jack preferred. She'd had it engraved: WITH LOVE FOR ALL TIME—HAYLEY.

To her surprise, Kelly's car was parked beside Jack's in front of the house. Hayley pulled into her space at the back of the driveway. What were those two up to? Had Jack planned a surprise of some kind?

Carrying the gift, Hayley climbed the wrought-iron staircase that led up the back of the house, to her apartment. She carefully opened her door. Everything inside seemed quiet.

"Jack?" Hayley called. "Kelly?"

No one answered. Hayley imagined them hidden in the living room, waiting to jump out with cries of "Surprise!". Who else would be there? Nick? Dinah? Roger? Maybe even Bruce.

The suspense was killing her. Laughing softly, Hayley walked down the long, dark hallway.

When she noticed the unraveled roll of crepe paper and a spilled bag of balloons, she began to feel a little uneasy. Jack was always so meticulous. He would never leave things lying around, especially if they'd give away a secret. Hayley stopped and picked up the balloons. They were wet. She turned on the hall light and saw blood staining her fingers.

"Jack? Kelly?"

Frantic, she ran into the living room. Crepe paper ran from the overhead light to each corner, giving the effect of a circus tent. Balloons bearing the legend HAPPY ANNIVERSARY had been hung everywhere, and there were stacks of party dishes on a table under the far window. But no sign of Jack and Kelly.

Slowly, Hayley moved into the room. One ray of crepe paper had fallen to the floor behind the couch. Following it, she found the end clutched tightly in Kelly's bloodied hand. Jack was slumped against the wall behind her, holding a fireplace poker as if he'd tried to defend himself. Blood had dried around a perfect hole in the middle of his forehead.

Hayley opened her mouth to scream, but a hand that smelled strongly of scotch clamped over it. She recognized Bruce Donner's voice as it rasped in her ear.

"What do you think of my little surprise?" he asked. "Do you like the way I decorated for us? I thought we could celebrate our trip to New York."

Hayley bit down hard on Bruce's palm. He let her go, and she ran screaming from the apartment. Her elderly downstairs neighbors threw open their door at her frantic pounding, nearly jumping out of the way as she stumbled into their apartment.

"He killed them," Hayley wailed, shaking like a leaf. "He killed Jack and Kelly!"

"What's she talking about?" Mrs. Markham asked her husband.

"You just calm her down, Elinor," said Mr. Markham. "I'm calling the police."

"He shot them! He shot them!"

Footsteps thumped down the staircase outside the apartment door. Through the Markhams' sheer white curtains, Hayley saw Bruce race into the street. He had to be looking for her.

"Stop him!" she shouted. "He's getting away!"

"Easy, dear, easy," Elinor said, holding her firmly.

Mr. Markham hung up the phone and said, "The police are on their way, Miss Seagel. Do you want to tell us what happened?"

Hayley had always been charmed by the way the old man insisted on calling her "Miss Seagel." Now his formality had a calming effect, and she was able to gain control. Before she could say much about finding her friends' bodies, sirens filled the air. Bruce, still searching the street, was surrounded by cops and lead away in handcuffs. He saw Hayley, watching from the Markhams' doorway, and turned to her, his eyes pleading for forgiveness.

"I did it for you," he said. "They didn't love you the way I do! They wanted to keep you from your career! *I killed them for you, Hayley!*"

Stunned, Hayley burst into tears again. Mrs. Markham tried to soothe her, but she would have none of it. It wasn't until the police sergeant came to question her that she finally calmed down enough to talk.

"I didn't know Bruce was really in love with me," she said. "I thought we were just friends."

"It's not your fault," the sergeant said. "What happened was not your fault."

"Could I . . . could I talk to him?" Hayley asked. "I

know it's a strange request, but I have to know what was going on inside his head."

"I'd have to see . . ."

"Please," she whispered.

The sergeant ran his fingers through his hair, wincing a little.

"I'll see what I can do, miss," he said.

At the police station, Hayley waited, pacing, in a small office. She was beyond tears for the moment, too numbed to cry. When the sergeant came back and told her she could try to talk to Bruce, she followed him silently.

"He doesn't have much to say to us," the cop said. "We're keeping him in a holding cell."

Hayley hoped she would have the strength to face Bruce, to question him calmly without thinking of what he'd done to Jack and Kelly, but she knew that was impossible. The most she could hope for would be a sort of clinical detachment, because that was the only way she could stop herself from flying at him, punching him, digging her nails into his eyes, ripping out his hair . . .

The violent reverie made her heartbeat quicken, and by the time they reached the cells, Hayley's hands were balled into tight fists. She took a few long breaths to relax herself. She just couldn't attack Bruce, as much as she hated him at that moment.

"You ready?"

She looked at the cop and nodded. He unlocked a door and led her into a short hall. Another officer unlocked a second, solid metal door. Hayley's footsteps echoed off the cement walls. It was very quiet, almost surreal in its lack of natural light and sound.

A few paces ahead of her, the sergeant stopped short. *"Damn!"*

"What's wrong?" Hayley demanded.

He tried to hold her back, but she pushed past him. Instantly, she saw what had caused his expletive. Bruce had hung himself from the lamp fixture over his cell, using a length of sheet as a noose.

As Hayley gazed in shock, his body swung slowly around. Bruce's eyes were open, and they seemed to stare into hers, their red rims a sickening contrast to the blue-white of his face.

"Oh, Bruce . . ." Hayley whispered.

"Come away, Ms. Seagel," the cop said. "This is no place for you."

Moving as if in a dream, Hayley brought her hand up and pointed at Bruce's chest. He'd taken off his shirt and carved a message into his flesh. Blood still dripped from a series of wounds that spelled:

"WAIT FOR ME."

Hayley knew the message was for her. But what did it mean?

Overcome, Hayley turned and raced down the hall, her heels echoing like gunshots. The place was filling with cops. Someone called to her, but she kept running until she was out of the building. Collapsing onto the grass, Hayley retched. The world seemed to swim around her, too much light and color and noise. Too much to take without Jack, without Kelly.

Now she'd never know why Bruce had murdered her best friend, why he'd taken her beloved Jack away from her.

She'd never see any of them again.

1

Hayley came around the edge of a jetty, her jogging feet stamping deep impressions in the sand. She veered to avoid stepping on a stranded jellyfish that lay like a round glass stone just above the waterline. The beach was quiet at this early morning hour, her favorite time to run. It was a chance to think and plan.

Today her thoughts were edged with melancholy. It had been five years since that horrible afternoon when she'd found Jack Langley and Kelly Palmer murdered by Bruce Donner. For a long time she'd felt responsible for their deaths, believing she should have seen the danger in Bruce's infatuation with her. Her dreams had been haunted by visions of Bruce's hanging body, and the bloodied words he'd etched into his chest. "WAIT FOR ME." She'd thought it was proof he was insane. Nobody could plan to come back from the dead. But in the past five years, memories of other strange events in her life had made her wonder.

When she was eleven years old, Hayley, her brother, and some neighborhood kids had been playing kickball when Hayley had suddenly begun to feel strange. Her stomach seemed to turn into a rock, and she grew very, very cold. The houses around her seemed to be alive, moving like gelatin. She did not understand what was happening, and she was terribly afraid that something bad was about to occur.

Without warning, a pickup truck barreled around the corner. The other children ran, screaming, but Hayley's brother Ricky stood frozen as the truck bore down on him. The ball he had just kicked was still rolling when the truck hit him, throwing him thirty feet. He died that night in the hospital, his parents holding both his hands.

For a long time after that, Hayley associated any ball with the image of her brother flying through the air. The sight of a game on television would send her into hysterics. It didn't matter that everyone told her she was too far away from Ricky to have helped him. It meant nothing that her parents insisted she was completely innocent. Hayley, sensing the strange feeling she'd had before the accident should have helped her save Ricky, became more and more withdrawn. Her parents did what they could to help her, but they were also grieving. They didn't even have the satisfaction of knowing who had killed their son. The hit-and-run driver had escaped.

Then, one Saturday morning about two months later, Hayley came into the kitchen with a smile on her face and said:

"USA 560."

"What?" her mother had asked, confused.

"USA 560," Hayley said again, sounding proud. "That

was the license plate of the truck. I couldn't remember it until now. But I had a dream, and I saw it."

"You can't be sure of that," her father said.

Hayley's face fell, and she seemed about to cry. Her mother put aside the pot she was washing and quickly came to her.

"Why not tell the police?" Hayley's mom said. "They could run a check on it . . . just to be sure."

"Well . . ."

David Seagel had given up all hope of seeing justice done in his son's death. But Hayley seemed so desperate to be believed that he made the call. He was outside trimming the hedges when Betty called to him.

"She was right," his wife said. "Hayley was right!"

When confronted, the pickup's driver admitted to his crime. Hayley didn't know if he'd gone to jail, or for how long. But catching him had been enough. Ricky could finally rest in peace.

She'd never told her parents that Ricky had given her the license number. She never told anyone that he'd appeared next to her bed, an ethereal form she could see right through. Strangely, she wasn't afraid of him, though she was too shocked to speak.

"I like it over here, Hayley. It doesn't hurt. And I'm not mad at you."

Hayley continued to stare.

"The truck had a number," Ricky went on. *"USA 560."*

At last, Hayley found her voice:

"Why didn't you come sooner, Ricky?"

"USA 560," Ricky said again, then disappeared.

She never saw him again.

The incident had become a distant memory over the years. Now it was like a vague dream. Hayley wasn't sure it had really happened.

Little by little, Hayley came out of the depression that had possessed her after the murders in Boston. She would never completely forget what had happened. Her love for Jack made it difficult to become serious with anyone else. She dated a few times over the years, but nothing ever came of it.

For some years, Hayley had lived in a small house on a Long Island beach. It had been in her family for years, and thoughts of happier childhood times had lured her back after the murders. That summer had felt so peaceful that she'd decided to stay. Now, when she occasionally wondered about the message Bruce had cut into himself, memories of Jack's hugs or Kelly's friendly smiles, made her strong again. She was experienced enough to know people *could* come back after death, but she also believed that Jack and Kelly would never let her be hurt.

Reaching her home, Hayley climbed an exterior staircase to the rooftop deck her father had had built so the family could sit up there and gaze out at the Atlantic Ocean. A refreshing breeze blew through her hair as Hayley did cool-down stretches. She watched a single boat drifting by in the distance, its sail scraping the horizon. Jack had had a small sailboat, and she'd played the part of first mate on many weekends.

Even after five years, she couldn't think of Jack and Kelly without feeling heat behind her eyes. She fought the sensation now and went back downstairs.

Her father had converted the little house to a year-round home long before he and her mother retired to North Carolina. Hayley had decorated it simply, with a hint of romance. Many of the pieces of furniture were white wicker, with fat striped cushions. Big bows on the curtains and the backs of the chairs added a feminine touch. Splashes of Hayley's favorite color, purple, appeared in flowered pillows, along the border of a big oval throw rug, and at the bases of two ginger jar lamps.

She showered quickly and dressed, getting ready to go out for brunch with Kate Reising. A friend since childhood, Kate had given Hayley a lot of support after Jack's death. She'd stayed with Hayley almost constantly when she'd arrived on Long Island. Kate had also lined up Hayley's first piano students when her friend mentioned her need to make money.

Teaching piano had proved to be a good idea, and now Hayley had twenty students a week. Those earnings, plus what she got from the investments she'd made with the money from "By Blood or by Marriage," were more than enough on which to get by. The show had closed for a few weeks of mourning. Then the cast had gone back to work, with a replacement director and a new actress in Kelly's part. The play ran for nearly another year in Boston, and had since been produced in several other cities—though not New York.

Arranging to meet, Kate had said she had an exciting idea to discuss with Hayley. An hour later, she and Kate were enjoying meals of swordfish steaks and Caesar salads at The Dockside Inn, seated beside a huge aquarium. Kate was wearing a dress of yellow and blue paisley, as bright as one of the tropical fish that swam lazily through plastic seaweed. With her big brown eyes and full lips, she resembled Liza Minelli—though with lighter brown hair.

"So, what's your idea?" Hayley urged.

Kate finished a mouthful of buttery swordfish before speaking.

"Have you seen all the publicity for mystery dinner theater?"

"Sure," Hayley said. "A company puts on a small

mystery production at various restaurants. The audience tries to guess 'whodunit.' "

"Right," Kate said, "and we get to put on a play that doesn't take weeks of practice. Best of all, we get paid for it."

"We?"

"I want you to start a company of your own, Hayley," Kate said. "It's the perfect way to come back to the theater again."

"I'm not ready . . ."

"You've been saying that for years!" Kate replied. "Hayley, I know different people take different amounts of time to grieve. But you're letting your life turn into a big nothing. I mean, what do you *do* all day? You don't have that many piano students—I know you've got hours of free time every day. Maybe it's hard to do things that remind you of Jack and Kelly, but this could be their legacy."

Hayley stared at the aquarium, watching a bright green and white fish undulate slowly through the water. Frankly, she had begun to miss the theater a few years earlier. But the idea of starting up a company like the one she'd had with Bruce seemed overwhelming. Kate's idea was a good one: a small troupe performing at local restaurants rather than in a theater. It could work . . .

"I'll have to sleep on it," she said.

"Great," Kate said. "From you, that's as good as a yes. We can try it once, and if it doesn't work, you can go back to doing whatever it is you do all day."

"Not so fast," Hayley cautioned her. "I haven't said 'yes' yet."

That night as she lay in bed, Hayley decided to go ahead. On the fifth anniversary of her loss, she dedicated her new company's success to the memory of Jack

Langely and Kelly Palmer. She even came up with a name that honored them both: Jackal Mystery Productions.

Two weeks later, thanks to an ad run in the local weekly flyer and several nights and weekends of auditions, they had their company.

2

*F*ive years. He'd begged her to wait for him, written it in his very blood, but in the blink of an eye she'd pushed aside all memory of Boston. Just five lousy years. She'd turned into a New York snob, laughing at him, mocking his love for her.

It was a good thing the other one had come to New York from Boston, and had recognized Hayley's name in the newspaper ad. A better thing that he'd changed so much that Hayley didn't recognize him. And, best of all, he was a good actor, able to pass the audition for Jackal Mystery Productions.

Laughing, low and secretive, the man went over to the mirror that hung near the front door. Hell, he didn't recognize himself. In life, he'd been much more robust than this little wimp. But he'd been searching for a way to get to New York, and when he heard of this man's plans, he'd decided to 'bum a ride.'

He laughed a little louder at the strange expression. Who'd have thought you could hitchhike in a body? And do such a good job of it that much of the body's own memories were lost? He'd had to erase all memories of Boston, or else Hayley might find out what was going on before the job was done. It was a big job, too. Might take a long time, but he'd enjoy every minute of it. Oh, yes, he'd enjoy every second *of making Hayley pay for not waiting. One by one, he'd take the lives of those around her. Unless she was stupid, it wouldn't take her long to get his message.*

He laughed even louder now, strange sounds that bounced around the room like a thousand demons screaming. He laughed until he doubled over, until the downstairs neighbors banged on their ceiling. Then he collapsed, exhausted, and for a time he gave the body, but not the memories, back to the kid.

Now that she was in the theater business again, albeit in a small way, Hayley realized how much she'd missed it. Kate had come over to work out some details with her over dinner. Hayley was tending to a delicate sauce, humming a tune, when the phone rang. Kate answered it, her voice animated. Hayley gave her friend a questioning glance, wondering who was on the phone. When Kate hung up, she put a hand on her chest as if to steady her heartbeat.

"Oh my God," she said breathlessly. "That was Wayne Boyer!"

"Who's that?"

"Oh, Hayley," Kate said with a little impatience. "Don't you read? Wayne Boyer's a mystery writer. I *love* his work. He wants to work for Jackal."

Hayley carried the vegetables to the table. Kate got up and retrieved the steaks, then poured iced tea.

"Never heard of him," Hayley said.

"He's the best," Kate said. "This is a great break for us. If we tell the restaurant owners we've got Wayne Boyer writing for us, we're sure to get a lot of bookings. He was on the *New York Times* bestseller list!"

Hayley busied herself, cutting her steak.

"You don't seem very impressed," Kate said. She sounded disappointed.

"I'm sure he'll be an asset," Hayley said, "if you say so. But I don't see why a best-selling author would want to write for a little unknown company like ours."

"Don't worry so," Kate said. "Look at it as a good sign."

"I'll do that when I see his work," Hayley replied. "Is he coming tomorrow night?" Jackal's first rehearsal would be at her house.

"I'm not sure," Kate said. "He said he'd try, but he might have other plans."

"Well, excuse us!" Hayley drawled. "He sounds stuck-up."

"Hayley . . ."

"Okay, okay," Hayley said placatingly. "I shouldn't judge a man before I meet him, right? Besides, we already have a first play to work on. Aidan McGilray sent me a really funny script."

"Ooh, that Aidan was something, wasn't he?" Kate said. "I was so impressed when he read for us during auditions. He's so cute, Hayley."

Hayley looked her friend straight in the eye.

"Don't even think about it, Katherine," she said. "No match-making!"

Kate leaned back, hands up.

"I won't!" she said. "When you call me Katherine, I know you mean business!" She tasted a carrot, then said softly: "But I still think he's cute."

* * *

Aidan *was* handsome, Hayley thought as he came into her house, wearing a wildly colored shirt open over a T-shirt, with a pair of loose-fitting jeans and Etonic sneakers. His brown hair was cut stylishly short. His smile was friendly, and there was a sparkle in his dark eyes.

Jack's eyes used to twinkle like that . . .

Hayley felt guilty immediately, and pushed away all admiring thoughts of Aidan. She turned her attention to short, balding Andy Constantino, who, at sixty, was the senior member of the group.

"Andy used to work in radio," Hayley told the others, recalling his resumé.

"WDEM," Andy said. "We broadcast a weekly mystery show that ran right through to the mid-fifties. It was great. We had some big guest stars."

Twenty-eight-year-old Sean Crane sidled up to them and encouraged Andy to continue.

"I love to listen to old radio recordings," he said. "I think I like 'The Shadow' best, but 'Inner Sanctum' runs a close second."

"I'll have to lend you one of my tapes," Andy said, his pale blue eyes beaming with pride.

Sean grinned. "I'd like that."

Hayley was about to ask Andy if he knew any celebrities when soft laughter made her look across the room. Aidan was standing with the youngest member of the company, twenty-four-year-old Hana Musashi. The Japanese girl had made such an impression at her audition that Hayley had at once chosen her for Jackal. With her pretty smile and ebony pageboy haircut, she'd probably play many an ingenue. Hayley excused herself from the group and went to talk to Hana and Aidan.

"I was admiring your unusual end table," Aidan said,

pointing to a rum barrel that held up a circle of smoked glass. "Hana doesn't believe that we had pirates in Long Island waters many years ago," he continued. "I told her that barrel could have been brought in by a rumrunner."

Hayley smiled.

"That's what my grandfather used to say," she answered. "The barrel's been in my family for generations. Grandpa Mulduar told me it was confiscated from a rumrunner."

She looked at Hana.

"But I just think it washed ashore one day," she said. "There's nobody that colorful in my family tree!"

"Oh, we all have interesting relatives," Aidan said. "How long has your family been in Montauk?"

"We've owned the house since I was little," Hayley said. "But my family's been here for years. Did you know that this area was used to quarantine people after the Spanish-American War? My great-great-grandfather stayed here in 1898, along with Teddy Roosevelt."

"Wow," Hana said.

The doorbell rang. When Kate opened the door, a tall, attractive woman entered. Hayley was surprised to see a baby carrier dangling from her long arm. Julianna Wilder gave everyone an apologetic smile.

"I'm sorry I had to bring the baby," she said, "but my husband isn't feeling well. I didn't want to miss our first rehearsal."

"Oh, that's okay," Hayley said.

Everyone gathered around the baby. Aidan knelt, letting the baby wrap her hand around his finger.

"Hello, cutie," he said. He looked up. "What is it?"

Kate laughed. "Can't you tell? It's a girl! Boys don't wear pink and lavender."

"Who's to say, these days?" Andy put in.

"Her name is Taylor," Julianna said. "She won't be

any bother, I promise. It's just that it's been so long since I worked in the theater, and this was the first night . . ."

Hayley didn't want the woman to ramble on, so she said quickly: "That's right, you used to be a Rockette."

Sean gazed at Julianna with admiration in his eyes.

"You worked on the stage at Radio City Music Hall?" he asked. "That's always been a dream of mine."

Hayley had to suppress an amused expression. Sean looked like a little kid with a crush. Not that she could blame him. Julianna was beautiful. Even in a comfortable jogging suit, it was easy to see that Julianna Wilder had a perfect dancer's body. She wore her blond hair pinned up, wisps of it curling around her forehead as if to point to her blue eyes.

"Well, we're all here," Hayley said. "Let's get started."

"What about Wayne?" Kate asked.

"Since he isn't acting in the plays," Hayley said, "he won't miss anything. Aidan's written a very funny play," Hayley continued. "The title is *Snake Eyes*. It takes place in a gambling casino."

She gave Aidan a quick smile. The brief smile he gave her in return made her heart flutter. Hayley busied herself passing out copies of the play and managed to overcome the momentary bout of infatuation.

The doorbell rang again, and Kate rushed to answer it, saying, "That must be Wayne Boyer!"

Wayne wasn't what Hayley had expected. Her mind conjured up the stereotypical image of a chiseled face hidden behind dark glasses. But Wayne's features were somewhat soft, giving him a boyish appearance despite his gray hair. He waved briefly as he walked in.

"Good evening, everyone," he said.

"Hi," was all Kate could say. Her eyes were huge.

Hayley kept her amusement to herself. Kate was acting like a smitten fan.

Sean came forward and took Wayne's hand, pumping it up and down.

"Welcome, Mr. Boyer," he said. "I'm so honored to work with you!"

"This is Sean Crane," Hayley said. She introduced everyone, finishing with, "And I'm Hayley Seagel. Welcome to Jackal Mystery Productions."

"Thanks," Wayne said, settling onto a bar stool in the corner. "I'll just sit back and observe, if you don't mind."

Hayley nodded and opened up her copy of the script.

"I thought Julianna could play the 'woman of mystery'," she began. "Andy, would you like to be the blackjack dealer?"

"Sounds good to me," Andy said.

"Kate does a perfect German accent," Hayley said, "so I think she'd be just right as the crazy psychiatrist, and Sean can be her patient, who's trying to overcome his need to gamble."

A short time later, all roles assigned, they began rehearsing. They worked for several hours, until Taylor began to fuss and Julianna announced it was time for them to go.

Andy said, "I think we had a good first night."

"Once we finished laughing and got down to business," Kate said.

"It was a very funny script," Wayne said.

Something in his tone sounded patronizing to Hayley, but she was too tired to care.

"I have a great idea," Julianna said as she zipped up Taylor's jacket. "Why don't we rehearse at my house? I have a huge basement where I practice my routines."

Hayley was excited.

"That sounds wonderful!" she said. "It *is* a little cramped in here. How about Saturday?"

"Fine."

Everyone exchanged good-byes and left. Hayley stood at the front door for a long time, looking up at the stars. She felt energized. If tonight was any indication of the future of Jackal, then she knew she could look forward to success. She had to admit Kate was right—it felt good to be working in theater again.

3

Kate's home was a three-room apartment in a complex about twenty miles west of Montauk. She'd been living alone for nearly two years, since her last boyfriend had taken off with another woman. Tony had left behind a lot of nice things—lamps and books and even an expensive desk they'd both picked out when they found this little place. Her friends had told her to get rid of all these constant reminders of the guy who jilted her. But Kate kept them, throwing away only his pictures and everything that had his writing on it. The mundane black desk set Tony had left was replaced with a brightly colored blotter and pen holder. Down came prints of hunting scenes and flying geese; up went reproductions of Renoir and other Impressionists.

She'd lived alone long enough now to feel comfortable with it, yet, for some reason, she'd felt uneasy from the moment she'd walked into her apartment tonight. She imagined this was how people felt when they thought they were being followed—a tingling at the back of her neck, a chill up and down her arms.

"Don't be stupid," she said to herself. "The door was locked tight."

Still, she moved carefully through her apartment, checking to see if anything had been disturbed. But every picture hung correctly, every knickknack sat in its proper place. It took all of two minutes to confirm that she was completely alone.

Alone. She was used to it, but that didn't mean she had to like it. Maybe she shouldn't have pushed Aidan at Hayley—maybe she needed someone for herself.

"Not my type," she said aloud.

For a split second, Kate was sure someone would answer her. Of course, no one did.

"Wishful thinking," she said.

As she prepared for bed, the strange feeling of being watched stayed with her, but she reasoned she was merely overtired. After all, she'd gone straight from her job at the Captain's Chair, an antiques store, to Hayley's. She just needed a rest.

When Kate was small, she'd sometimes thought a faceless man, perhaps a demon, was lurking beneath her bed, ready to grab her little bare foot if it dared creep out from beneath her covers. Over the years, she'd forgotten that fear, and never gave much thought to the fact that she kept her top sheet tucked in all around the bottom of her mattress.

Sometime after midnight, Kate rolled over in her sleep, and her foot jutted out over the edge of the bed. This was so unexpected a situation, after so many years of being tucked in, that she woke. She lay there drowsily for a short while, staring at her own foot until she realized what had happened. Somehow, the covers had come undone.

Kate couldn't remember that ever happening before. She pulled in her foot and sat up. She looked at the end of the bed. The covers weren't just undone a little. They were as crumpled as if she'd been tossing and turning for hours.

She snapped on the bedside lamp.

The room was empty, very still and quiet except for the sound of the filter humming in the fish tank near the window. She watched her pair of angelfish drift lazily through the water, probably asleep.

"Must have had a wild dream," she said out loud.

Kate pushed her covers aside and swung around to put her feet on the floor. No sooner had she stood up than something shot out from beneath the bed and grabbed her ankle. With a cry of dismay, Kate slammed to the floor as her leg was pulled under the bed. Terrible fear crashed over her, unnamed fear that only her subconscious remembered from her long-ago thoughts of the bogeyman. She knew only one thing as she struggled to get away: Someone was trying to kill her!

"Nnnnoooo!"

She grabbed at the leg of her nightstand and held fast.

"I've got you now," a man's voice said. "I've got you."

The voice didn't yell, didn't even sound angry. It was strangely calm and matter-of-fact. Somehow, that was more frightening than any emotional threat.

"Let me go!" Kate shouted, trying to pull away.

Looking toward her foot, she saw that the hand that was wrapped around her ankle was so pale it seemed blue. Its iron grip was terribly painful.

Summoning all her strength, Kate twisted onto her side. She'd tried kicking the man's hand away, but the impact of her small bare foot had no effect. Now, she braced it against the bed and pushed as hard as she could.

"Let . . . me . . . go . . . you . . . friggin' . . . *bastard*!"

Miraculously, her captive foot suddenly came free. Kate jumped up and stumbled out of the bedroom, not looking back as she ran for the phone near the front door. She was shaking so violently that she had to hang up and dial a second time. It wasn't until she was listening for a ring that never came that she realized the phone was disconnected.

She ran for the front door now, fumbling with the deadbolt while she kept one eye on her bedroom door. Where the hell was he? Why didn't he come out here? She heard the bolt click back and tried to open the door. It wouldn't budge. The lock on the knob! As her shaking hand grabbed at it, she heard footsteps behind her.

She dared to look around, to face her enemy.

What she saw was overwhelming. Her knees buckled.

It was the faceless man of her childhood nightmares. He was *real*, and he had waited thirty years to get her. This was worse than any dream—he was a walking shadow, a man-shaped hole in reality, pure darkness.

"Kate . . ." Of course he knew her name. The bogeyman knew everything about her.

"G-go away . . ." She whimpered like a small child.

"I'm not going to hurt you, Kate," he said in a surprisingly gentle voice. "I'm just here to warn you. Give up your friendship with Hayley. She doesn't deserve a friend like you. She didn't deserve a friend like Kelly. She's a hateful bitch. She didn't wait for me. No one should love her."

"Go away," Kate said again, her voice only slightly stronger.

"Stay away from Hayley, Kate, unless you want to join me."

The air made a strange sucking noise, and the shadow-man was pulled into another dimension. At the same time, Kate fell into her own blackness.

The sound of the phone ringing pulled Hayley out of a deep sleep. Groggily, she looked at her clock and cursed to see it was only 12:15 A.M. Who the hell was calling at this hour?

When she heard Kate's frantic voice on the answering machine, she ran to the phone.

"Kate!" she called into the line, "Kate, what's wrong!"

"He's after me!" Kate screamed. "The Shadow Man came for me! He was angry at you because you didn't wait for him, and now he wants to kill me because you're my friend!"

"Kate, you're not making sense," Hayley said, trying to calm her friend, to figure out what was going on. "Is someone there with you? Are you in danger?"

"Help me, Hayley!" Kate screamed. "Wait for him! Wait for him!"

"Wait for me . . ."

The voice came from behind her. Hayley swung around, phone in hand. The room was empty.

"Kate?" She spoke tremulously, her gaze darting about the room. Was someone hiding in here?

"Kate, talk to me," Hayley demanded.

The line was dead.

Hayley hung up and quickly dialed 911. A robotic voice came over the line.

"We're sorry," it said. "The number you have dialed is no longer in service. Please check . . ."

"How the hell can 911 be out of service?" Hayley demanded.

She slammed the receiver down and hurried into her

room to get dressed. She would drive to Kate's house to make certain her friend was all right.

All her drawers were empty.

"Where are my clothes?" she asked.

She looked up at the mirror, as if her reflection had an answer.

Jack was staring out at her. Kelly stood behind him, holding the strings of a bunch of black balloons in her hand. Jack was trying to say something, his bloodless mouth moving to form words. Frustration masked his pale but still-handsome face. Hayley stared at him, unafraid of the man she'd loved. He'd come back to her again! Slowly, she reached toward the glass . . .

A pale hand shot out from the mirror and grabbed her wrist. Jack and Kelly's images melted away to reveal the angry countenance of Bruce Donner.

"Why didn't you wait for me?" he demanded.

His grip tightened painfully around her wrist. Hayley began to scream . . .

. . . and found herself sitting upright in bed. She'd only been dreaming. Gasping for breath, she held a hand to her chest and felt her heart racing. It had been a long time since she'd had a nightmare about Bruce. What had brought it on tonight?

"Oh God," she said, the words more air than substance. "Oh God . . ."

It took her a long time to calm down. She half expected the phone to ring. Warily she glanced at her clock. Twelve-forty.

It would be nearly three A.M. before she fell asleep again.

As it had in her dream, the phone woke her the following morning. She lay in bed listening to the rings for a long time, until the answering machine picked up. Trying to decide if she was still dreaming, Hayley paid no attention to the caller. She felt hunger pangs, heard noises about the house.

"I'm awake," she said out loud, getting up.

She paused to look at the mirror, but saw only her own weary self. Running her fingers through her hair, she went to the answering machine and played back the message. As she half expected, it was Kate. She seemed upset about something, although not as hysterical as she'd been in the dream. Kate wanted to meet for breakfast.

It seemed like a nice idea. Hayley called Kate and they quickly set up a meeting place. A short time later, the women met in a little coffee shop on the beach. Round white tables were arranged on a deck under green-and-white striped umbrellas. There were few patrons present this early in the morning, giving the place a sense of privacy. Hayley arrived first and sat watching seagulls fight over scraps of toast that had been thrown to them. When Kate joined her, Hayley gave her friend a bright smile.

"We had a great time last night," Hayley said in greeting.

"Last night?" Kate seemed confused for a moment. "Oh, you mean at the rehearsal."

It wasn't like Kate to act befuddled, not even for a moment.

"Is something wrong?" Hayley asked.

"I had the weirdest dream last night," Kate said. "You know, the kind of dream that stays with you?"

"That's strange," Hayley said, "so did I. What was your dream about?"

Kate told her. As she listened, Hayley became increasingly disturbed. There was just too much coincidence.

"What time was this?"

Kate shrugged. "I don't know. Midnight, one A.M. Somewhere in there."

The clock had said 12:15 in Hayley's dream, when Kate had called her on the phone.

Had Kate tried to contact her, to warn her?

No, that was ridiculous.

"What are you thinking, Hayley? Tell me about your dream."

"It started with a ringing phone," Hayley said. "You were on the line, and you were very upset. You said someone wanted to kill you because you were my friend. I think I know who your Shadow Man was, Kate. Bruce Donner."

"Bruce Donner!" Kate echoed. "Why would I dream about him? I only met the guy once."

"You said he was mad because I didn't wait for him," Hayley said. "Kate, I've got to set something straight. Did I ever tell you about finding Bruce in the jail cell?"

Kate nodded, her expression grim.

"Did I tell you what he'd done to himself?"

"He hanged himself."

"No, I mean something else," Hayley said. She saw by Kate's questioning expression that she hadn't revealed the painful story of the cuts in Bruce's chest.

So how the hell had Kate dreamed that Bruce wanted her to wait for him?

"I don't know what to make of this," Hayley said. "It's really a great coincidence."

"What else happened to Bruce?" Kate asked, concern in her voice.

Hayley shook her head slightly. "I'd rather not say right now. I don't like to think about it."

She concentrated on her scrambled eggs and hash browns for a while. Kate chewed on a piece of bacon and stared out the window, thoughtful. Then she leaned forward, as if ready to share a secret.

"I think I understand," she said. "It's a theory, at least.

We're both very excited about starting Jackal. You dedicated the company to the memory of Jack and Kelly. They represent good."

"And Bruce?"

"I didn't really dream of Bruce," Kate said. "I dreamed of the bogeyman, the Shadow Man. I think he represented my fears that things might go wrong."

Hayley's eyebrows went up.

"You? Afraid something might go wrong?"

"What? Me worry?" Kate quoted *Mad* magazine's famous character. "Of course I worry, Hayley. We'll be investing a lot of time and money in Jackal. Things can always screw up. You dreamed of Bruce because he signifies disaster in your mind." Kate looked down at the table. "With good reason.

"But we both dreamed at the same time," Hayley said. "And we both dreamed that someone wanted me to wait. 'Wait for Me'—that was the message Bruce . . . left for me before he died."

Kate was thoughtful again.

"You know," she said, "you probably did tell me that, and I just forgot it. Starting Jackal reminded us both of your old Boston company, and made us both dream."

Hayley had to admit it made sense. It was better than thinking something bad had happened.

"Good old Kate," she said. "Always looking at the logical side of things."

"Must be the Vulcan in me," Kate said dryly.

Hayley couldn't help a laugh. She let Kate's reasoning and good humor squash her misgivings. They changed the subject to something more pleasant. But all the while, deep in her subconscious, a familiar voice was warning Hayley that something was very, very wrong.

Almost like an omen, a seagull landed on the railing right beside their table. Kate laughed.

"Cocky little guy, isn't he?" she asked.

The bird turned its head toward Kate.

"Look at that," Kate said. "You'd think he understood me."

"Of course he doesn't," Hayley said. "He's just following the sound of your voice. Shoo! We don't have anything for you!"

The bird turned and seemed to stare at Hayley.

"Oh, don't be stingy," Kate said, breaking off a piece of muffin. "Here, fella. Here ya go!"

"Kate . . ."

Hayley saw the bird's eyes suddenly turn flaming red. It screeched loudly, then grabbed at both the muffin and Kate's finger. Kate screamed, jumping back in her chair.

The gull held on, its beak like a vise around Kate's finger. Blood spattered all over the white tablecloth as Kate tried to shake the bird away.

"Get it off me!" she cried, shaking her hand. *"Get it off!"*

A waiter rushed out of the restaurant.

"Help her!" Hayley commanded, leaping to her feet.

The waiter looked stunned. Then he half-tripped, half-ran back inside. Kate kept screaming. The gull's beak was clamped to her hand. The other patrons stared in shock. One man finally had the sense to try to hit the bird away, using a rolled-up newspaper. The seagull shrieked and let go, flying at the man, beak and claws ready to attack. He leaped back, then ran away. The bird jumped onto a nearby table and paced there, beak snapping, eyeing the women and crying. Kate stared at it. She held her wounded hand high; blood dripped down her forearm.

"What the hell is happening?" she demanded.

"Kate, let's get out of here," Hayley said.

Kate started to stand up. The seagull, as if on a vendetta, suddenly dove at her with a screech. Its claws

scraped across the top of her head as she ducked, screaming. The bird shot past the women, then looped around.
Holding on to Hayley, Kate did not try to get up again.
The bird flew closer, threatening, but did not attack. Hayley threw a glass at it. The gull avoided it neatly and
called again. It seemed to be laughing at Hayley.

"My God," Kate said, "I'd swear that thing is following me!"

"We've got to get you some help," Hayley said worriedly, wrapping a napkin around Kate's hand.

The waiter finally came back, armed with a seltzer
bottle. The manager came, too, broom in hand. They
bombarded the maddened seagull, spraying and hitting it
until it finally collapsed, dead, in a heap of blood and
feathers.

The manager took off his white cap and ran a hand
through his hair. The young waiter stood wide-eyed.

"Been here thirty years," the manager said. "Never
saw anything like that."

"There's . . . there's a first-aid station two doors
down," the waiter said.

"I know," Hayley answered, helping Kate to her feet.

Kate had wrapped a fresh white napkin around her
hand, replacing the blood-soaked one. Hayley tried to
pay the bill, but the manager said breakfast was on the
house and stared after the women as they left.

"That bird attacked me on purpose," Kate said, voice
shaking.

"It seems that way," Hayley agreed. *Almost as if he
were possessed.*

"Something sure pissed him off," Kate said. "I guess
any animal can go wild."

At the first-aid station, the lifeguard on duty washed
the wound and wrapped it carefully. He sent Kate away
with a warning to have her doctor look at it.

Kate, never one to dwell on the bad side of life, insisted she was fine.

"It just pounds a little," she said.

Nonetheless, Hayley walked with her to the Captain's Chair, the shop where Kate worked.

"Please, Kate," she said, "see your doctor. I don't know if birds carry diseases, but don't take a chance."

"I promise, I will," she said. "You know, Hayley, between last night's dream and this crazy incident, I think I've had all the weird stuff I can take for a while."

"You and me both," Hayley agreed.

Kate opened the antique shop's door. The jingling bell punctuated her quick farewell wave. Hayley turned and walked away, still feeling uneasy. The way that bird had looked at her—could those red eyes have just been a reflection of the sun?

Or was it something more?

She quickened her pace to her car, unaware that she was hunching her shoulders as if afraid of being attacked herself.

4

Everyone agreed to meet at Hayley's on Friday night. Sean was the first to arrive, dressed in shorts and an Izod shirt and sunburned from a day on the beach.

"Hi!" he said brightly as he entered the house.

"You sound happy," Hayley said. "Are you ready to work?"

"Got my lines memorized," Sean said. "I was lying on the beach reading them."

Andy came next, with a bakery box in one hand and a shopping bag in the other.

"Italian pastries," he said. "I passed a nice bakery on the way."

"A man after my own heart," Kate said. "I *love* Italian pastries!" She took the box into the kitchen. Andy came over to Hayley, who was fluffing a cushion.

"I've got something even better than pastries," he told

her. "Props! I played Nicely Nicely in a production of *Guys and Dolls* many years ago, and I thought, since this was a play about gambling, we could use some of my souvenirs."

"That sounds perfect," Hayley said, trying to peek into the bag as Andy set it down beside the couch.

The doorbell rang, and Hayley answered it and greeted Wayne Boyer.

"I've got the outline for our next play," he said, handing Hayley a manila envelope.

"Wonderful!" Hayley said. "What's it about?"

"It takes place—"

The doorbell interrupted him. Hana came in looking terribly upset.

"Almost got run off the road," she said, nearly breathless, "but I'm okay."

"Hana, are you sure?" Hayley asked, worried. "You aren't hurt at all?"

Hana smiled reassuringly. "I'm fine, really," she insisted. "Just a little out of breath."

Aidan and Julianna arrived one after the other a few moments later. Julianna's baby swung in her carrier, a sweet face showing in a bundle of pink blanket.

"Jamie's still sick," she said. "I didn't want to make him take care of Taylor."

"It's okay," Hayley said, though only halfheartedly. She hoped this wasn't going to become a habit. A crying baby could be very disruptive.

Wayne rolled his eyes and busied himself at the liquor cart. Everyone else made a fuss over the baby, until Hayley said it was time to begin rehearsal.

"Andy brought some props," she said. "Let's see what we can use."

Andy displayed his treasures—giant dice and playing

cards, lamps shaped like suits of the deck, and a red bow tie that lit up with tiny lights.

"Aidan should wear that, as the dealer," Hayley said. Aidan took the tie and fastened it around his neck.

"I put batteries in it," Andy said. He showed Aidan the hidden button that turned on the lights; Aidan pressed it, and the tie lit up. Everyone applauded.

"Thanks, Andy," Hayley said. "We can really use these."

Although the group had only met once before, it was a smooth night, and they accomplished a lot. Hayley was happy to see her company was starting off on a very professional foot. If the dreams she and Kate had had represented their fears, this rehearsal reassured her that things would be all right.

While people were getting ready to leave, Aidan went to the sliding door and looked out at the stars. Moonlight reflected off the ocean in sparkling dabs of silver.

"I could get into working in a place like this," he said. "The sound of the ocean nearby would be inspiring."

"It would make me want to run out for a swim," Sean said.

"As a writer," Wayne said, "I prefer no distractions at all. But of course, Aidan, we all have our own ways to create."

"Oh, I'm not a writer," Aidan admitted. "I design video games. I came up with the idea for this little skit from one of my projects."

"Wow!" Sean said. "Maybe I've played some of your games!"

Aidan shrugged. "You might have. I've had marginal success in the field."

"Maybe you'll have better success as a writer," Hayley said.

Aidan gave her a surprised look. She understood why.

Except for the business of rehearsing, she had all but ignored him all night. Hearing her praise him must have been completely unexpected. It had surprised Hayley to say it, and now she felt uncomfortable. Aidan was looking at her steadily. Wayne had turned away. Hayley could see that he was ill at ease. She wondered if he felt bad because someone else had written the first skit for Jackal Mystery.

Before she could say anything, Wayne changed the subject.

"It doesn't bother you to live alone, Hayley?" he asked. "I mean, in such an isolated place, the way things are today."

"Not at all," Hayley said. "I like the peacefulness, the sound of the waves nearby. My apartment in Boston was on a very busy street. This is heaven, compared to that."

"You can't live in fear," Sean said.

"He's right," Aidan agreed. "But these days, you've got to know how to defend yourself."

"Hana's resume says she knows karate," Hayley commented, wanting to get the spotlight off herself.

Hana smiled shyly. "Only a green belt."

"Really?" Wayne said. "I'll have to work that into another play."

"I'm a kung fu man myself," Aidan said. "I've been studying since I was a kid. You know, Hayley, they teach an excellent self-defense course at my dojo."

"Why don't you sign up?" Kate asked. "It sounds like fun."

Hayley shot Kate a quick, warning glance. She knew her friend was trying to push her at Aidan.

"Why is everyone so concerned about my safety?" she demanded.

"I think we were just talking about being alone," Sean said. "And it led up to this."

"I'm just fine alone," Hayley insisted, giving Kate a pointed look. "Just fine."

"Well," Wayne said, shrugging into his jacket, "be sure you lock up."

Hayley nearly laughed aloud at his statement, so unusual for a man so very self-centered. Why the sudden concern for her? An hour later, when she was lying in bed reviewing her day, his words came back to her. In retrospect, it almost sounded like a warning of impending danger.

But that was ludicrous. It was just the solitude of the moment.

Impulsively, Hayley got up and went to find the little crystal mouse Jack had given her. She always drew such comfort from it, as if some of Jack's spirit was trapped within the shimmering leaded glass.

Holding the mouse firmly in one hand, she went to sit in the big overstuffed chair in the living room. Snuggling into pillows spattered with violets and ivy, she closed her eyes and tried to bring back a happy memory of Jack. That was the best way to push scary thoughts out of her mind.

Although they'd only had a short time together, she had so many sweet memories. One of her favorites came to mind now, a leisurely ride on Jack's boat. It had been a warm spring day, and Jack had just moved in with her that morning.

"It's going to be great," he said, being with you all the time."

Hayley had laughed. "Well, not all the time. You've got the lab—I've got the theater. But now I've got someone to come home to."

She turned her face up to his, sunshine warm on her skin. He kissed her softly. Then he put his arms around her and began to kiss her more passionately, his fingers playing with the back of her bathing suit top. Hayley laughed and pushed him gently away.

"Not here," she whispered. "People on the other boats can see us."

"You're no fun."

"Yep, that's me," Hayley admitted. "One big bore when it comes to sex."

"This is not sex," Jack insisted. "Kissing is *not* sex."

Hayley tilted her head.

"Tell that to the old man in that sloop."

Jack looked beyond her.

"What old man?"

Hayley turned her head. The sloop was gone. They were the only ones on the water. She shook her head, frowning.

"I don't know what happened to him."

Jack put a hand on her cheek and turned her to face him. He looked different; the natural golden color of his skin had faded to a strange mint-greenish color. His lips were pale.

"But you know who he is," he said. "He was supposed to be there that day."

"What?"

"I . . ." Jack stopped talking. He waved his hands in futility, as if unable to get the right words out.

"He . . . won't let me tell you . . ." he gasped.

Someone was tapping Hayley on the shoulder. She turned to see Kelly Palmer, looking as pale as Jack. She was holding a bunch of black balloons. One popped . . .

. . . and suddenly Hayley was awake in the armchair. Her mind had taken her from a memory into a dream. Jack had been trying to tell her something, but couldn't. What did it mean? Why, after five years of only pleasant dreams of Jack, had she suddenly had two dreams of warning?

Jack had seemed very troubled about something, and frustrated that he couldn't tell her what it was.

"Who was stopping you, Jack?" Hayley whispered out loud.

Jack's disappointment had carried over into Hayley's waking self, leaving a sense of great futility. If only she could talk to him, as she had so long ago! If only she could understand! It had to be something important, something Jack *had* to tell her. Kelly had come, too, to warn her. She hadn't been there that day, when Jack and Hayley had gone boating. But she'd been in the dream. Why? The image of her friends' pale, troubled faces floated in Hayley's mind.

They'd looked almost like ... ghosts.

Because Jack and Kelly died together, they'll be connected forever.

Hayley understood that, but understanding didn't help her feel more comfortable. In fact, she grew more uneasy.

"Just a dream," she told herself, hoping the sound of her voice would reassure her.

Instead, she was colder, tenser.

Someone was in the house. She had locked the doors and windows, not because of what Wayne had said, but out of habit. Yet someone had managed to get in. She was as certain of this as if he were standing right in front of her.

That must be why Jack and Kelly had come. They wanted to warn her that she was in danger!

She rose quietly from the armchair. In the small house, there would be no dashing for the front door without being caught. She crept into the bathroom and locked the door. The tile walls had an insulating effect against sound, and all was quiet.

Then a footstep, creaking loudly on the floor.

Hayley caught her breath.

Someone's going to kill me.

The way Jack and Kelly had been killed. Maybe she'd been meant to die that day, too. Maybe she'd arrived a moment too late to be caught up in Bruce Donner's rage. And that was why Jack and Kelly had come to warn her.

"No," she whispered. "Bruce didn't want to kill me."

Her defensive instincts had kicked in; she was angry that her home was being invaded. She searched quickly for a weapon, choosing a can of hairspray and a curling iron. She might be able to spray the intruder's eyes, then jab him hard in the ribs. Holding her tools firmly, she left the bathroom and stormed through her bedroom.

"Who the hell are you?"

No answer but the ticking clock and the nearby waves of the Atlantic.

"Answer me!" she demanded, furious.

The curtains at the sliding glass doors moved just slightly. Hayley paced towards them, makeshift weapons at the ready. She kicked at the curtain, and her foot hit glass.

"Come out!"

No response. She told herself, very firmly, that she would be able to see the outline of a person behind the curtains. There was no one in her house.

But there might be someone outside, someone trying to get in. She reached for the outside light switch and turned on the patio lights. They glowed softly through the curtains.

"Get away from here!"

Soft scratching answered her.

Like an animal . . .

Had she been terrorized by a stray cat or dog? Hayley stood for a few moments, collecting her wits. That had to be it. Just the sounds of some poor mutt. She set her lips hard and gave the curtains a determined yank to the side.

There was a man outside, staring into her house.

No, not a man at all. A rat, a huge rat, filthy and ugly and hungry.

Few things in the world frightened Hayley more than rats.

She screamed, still clutching the curtains, as the rat frantically tried to scratch its way into the house. It had to be six feet tall. Its paws were as big as her hands. Its eyes glared with fury, staring directly at her, bright red with hatred. Bright red, like the seagull's eyes. Hayley tried to close the curtains, to turn away as the rat opened its slimy, dripping mouth. Blood stained its teeth, as if it had just devoured something.

As Hayley stared in dread, the blood-matted hairs on the thing's chest began to move around. Crazily, Hayley was reminded of a childhood toy where a magnet was used to move iron filings around a man's face. At last, the squirming hairs formed words, horribly familiar words.

WAIT FOR ME!

Hayley screamed, backing away, finally loosening her death grip on the curtains. They fell back into place, hiding the monstrosity outside. This was a dream! It had to be a dream! She just wanted that thing to go away, go away, go away . . .

She stumbled over a planter, and everything went black.

Sometime later, Hayley woke up on the dining room floor. She was still clutching the curling iron, but the hairspray had fallen to the floor. Hayley realized she'd been walking in her sleep. The curtains were drawn, the patio lights were out, and everything seemed normal.

She'd only dreamed of parting the curtains and seeing that horrid rat, but she felt as if it had been real.

Slowly, Hayley got to her feet. Like a woman possessed, she hurried around the small house, switching on lamps. It wasn't until the whole dwelling was bathed in bright light that she could be certain that she was completely alone. It had only been a case of nerves.

"I know I heard something," she told herself.

She hadn't sleepwalked since her brother's death.

Hayley sank down into an armchair. Aidan had said she seemed like a woman who could take care of herself. What would he think of her now? Why had she behaved in such a paranoid way? It was like the months right after Jack and Kelly were murdered, when she'd been suspicious of every noise and shadow.

"But not these days!" she said out loud. "I'm fine, now!"

In time, she grew drowsy again. The curling iron, clutched tightly in her hand, dropped to the floor as she relaxed. She was soon deeply asleep, and dreaming again of Jack and Kelly.

"You know who he is," Jack said. "He was supposed to be there that day."

When Hayley woke up in the morning, every light in the house was still burning brightly. She showered, dressed, and had breakfast quickly, wanting to get her day going, to forget what had happened last night. She was about to open the curtains at the sliding doors, when she froze, thinking of the rat she'd seen last night.

"Silly," she told herself. "There are no giant rats! It was only a dream!"

With that, she pulled open the curtains.

And gasped in horror to see a real rat, clearly dead, stuck to her window with packing tape. The words

TRAITOR BITCH were scrawled in blood across the glass.

Kate arrived at Hayley's house shortly after the police. She sat beside Hayley on the couch and watched as the fingerprint technicians worked around the back door. Hayley told her about the night's events, omitting only the message on the rat's chest.

"I gave a full statement to the police," Hayley said. She shuddered. "I felt so nervous. I could only think of the interrogation I went through after Jack and Kelly were murdered."

"This is nothing like that," Kate said, running a hand through her hair. The finger that had been bitten by the seagull was still bandaged. "You shouldn't feel afraid to talk to the police. But that rat! Now, that's something to be afraid of. It must have been horrible!"

"If they get any usable fingerprints, they'll check their files for any matches," Hayley said. "And they promised to have someone cruise by here for the next few nights. I'm supposed to tell them if anything else happens."

She sighed. "The officer asked me for a list of enemies. I couldn't tell her a single person. I don't know of anyone who hates me."

She looked out the window.

"It's strange," she said. "I had another dream of Jack and Kelly. Jack said the strangest thing. He said, 'You know who he is. He was supposed to be there that day.' I wonder what that means?"

Kate thought for a few moments, then asked, "Do you know what lucid dreaming is?"

"No."

"It's when a person is actually aware they're dreaming," Kate said. "Maybe that's what happened to you."

Hayley shrugged.

"I think," Kate went on, "that you might have heard some noise when that creep taped the rat to your window. You walked out here to investigate, half asleep, and in a dreamlike state you hallucinated the big rat when you saw that real one on your window."

Hayley considered this. It certainly made sense. God bless Kate for always making things seem better. She took a deep breath.

"Okay, then," she said. "I half dreamed a giant rat. I certainly don't believe it was really there!"

That last statement was practically a lie, but Hayley wouldn't let herself dwell on this. And she didn't wonder why she hadn't told Kate about the words that had formed in the rat's matted hair.

"You know," Kate said, "you could stay with me for a while."

"Thanks," Hayley said with a smile. "But I'm not being driven from my home. Summer vacation is just beginning. Maybe it was just a rowdy teenager."

"Rowdy isn't the word for it," Kate said, playing with her bandaged finger. "And why would some teenager call you traitor? Do you even know any teenagers?"

Hayley shook her head. She had some adult piano students, but no teens—the bulk of her pupils were children, the oldest about ten. It was just a theory, something to grasp because there was nothing that made sense.

Now she noticed Kate grimacing a little as she toyed with her injured finger. Hayley nodded toward it.

"Does that still hurt?"

"It stings," Kate said. "I changed the bandage this morning, and it still looked red."

"Maybe you should have it checked by a doctor," Hayley suggested.

"I will," Kate promised, "if it doesn't feel better by to-morrow."

Hayley nodded, approving. She didn't want anything to happen to Kate. She thought of the strange seagull, of the rat, and her weird dreams. Then she said a quick, silent prayer that they weren't portents of more trouble to come.

5

Wayne balled his hands into fists and slammed them down onto the keyboard, sending wild messages to the computer. It beeped loudly in protest, random letters scooting across the screen like a cartoonist's symbolic interpretation of swearwords: @*()#!

It was hard enough coming up with a good idea the first time around. Now he'd discovered that not only had the script been stolen, someone had come into the apartment and erased the copy from his hard drive—and he hadn't yet made a back-up copy. It was strange—there were no signs of forced entry, and nothing else was missing, not even the thick gold chain hanging on his mirror. The chain had been a gift from a fan, and Wayne kept it on display to remind himself that he really did have a following. He never wore it, considering such heavy gold chains ostentatious. If someone had been bent on robbing the place, that would have been the first thing taken. But there it hung, while a few pages of dialogue had vanished.

Why? Who the hell would want the darned thing? Sure, he was Wayne Boyer. His work brought in decent money; at least, it had once. Maybe someone didn't want him to start writing again. Maybe someone didn't want the competition. Maybe . . .

The doorbell rang. Turning off the computer, Wayne went to answer it. His eyebrows went up upon seeing a familiar face.

"What are you doing here at this hour?" he asked. "It's a long way . . ."

The man at the door held up a manila envelope.

Wayne looked at the man with delight in his eyes, but before he would say thank you he wanted to assure himself that his script was safe. How could he have missed a big envelope like this, lying in the street?

He unhooked the clasp and reached inside.

Something slithered across his hand.

"There's a snake in here!" he cried, throwing the package across the room. It slammed against the wall. "What the hell kind of joke is this?"

When he looked up, the man he knew was no longer there. A complete stranger stood in his place. No, there was something familiar about him. Wayne had seen that face before . . .

The man grabbed Wayne by the collar, pulling him close. A fetid smell, a strange mix of rotting meat, old leaves, and printer's ink spewed forth as the man hissed at him. Wayne gagged, trying to turn his head but unable to, imprisoned in his attacker's grip.

"Nobody writes for her now," the invader said. His eyes were jet-black, like pools of oil. Wayne could see his reflection in them. "Especially not a hack like you. You'll never be the writer I was!"

Effortlessly he picked up Wayne and threw him across the room. The novelist landed near the envelope he'd tossed away earlier. A yellow-and-red snake was trying to slither free of the package. Wayne scrambled away from the creature, terrified, but only succeeded in backing himself into a corner. He froze, watching the snake move across the carpet. Only his knees moved, shaking violently.

"Nobody!"

Wayne shut his eyes, but ice-cold fingers pulled them open again. He looked up at the stranger, frantic, as the snake crawled closer.

How could this man have known his fear of snakes? How could anyone know? He'd conquered it years ago, through expensive therapy. And yet here he was, reduced to a quivering mass by a small monstrosity that slithered closer and closer.

A silly poem came to mind:

"Red touch yellow, kill a fellow.

Red touch black, a friend to Jack."

The snake moved right toward him, as if it had a purpose in mind. Its tongue shot in and out of its mouth, tasting the scents in the air, searching for its victim. Wayne saw the adjacent red and yellow stripes and knew this snake was a killer. With a cry, he found the strength to jump up, over the back of the couch.

When he landed on the cushions, the snake was there.

"How the hell . . . ?"

The snake reared back and hissed at him, eyes glowing red. Wayne froze solid. Maybe if he didn't move . . .

As he stared at the reptile, his terrified mind couldn't understand how it had gotten onto the couch so quickly. And he only half-registered the fact that, somehow, the snake had grown. It had to be fifteen feet long, its tail coiled up over the back of the couch.

Fifteen feet long, but it had fit in a standard manila envelope.

"She didn't wait," the other man said, his voice distracted, as if Wayne wasn't there. "Why didn't she wait?"

"Why didn't *who* wait?" Wayne growled, summoning a tiny bit of bravery.

A hissing noise spun him back to face the snake, and his bravado vanished. The monster was thirty feet long now if it was an inch, looping over couch and armchair, its tail flicking against the wall.

"Dear God," Wayne moaned. "Get it away from me!"

"Frickin' hack," the stranger growled. "She's going to be sorry she didn't wait for me. I would have waited for her! I would have!"

"Get it away from me!"

Wayne screamed so loudly he was certain the neighbors would hear, summon the police, and save him. But he heard nothing. There would be no last-minute rescue.

Wayne screamed as the snake-thing snapped forward and hooked into his side. He screamed as its teeth sank into him, as it sucked his blood, as it writhed and coiled and wrapped itself around his body. He screamed as the convulsions set in.

His heart pounded, racing. The room seemed to expand and contract.

Finally the walls seemed to collapse around him, engulfing everything. Wayne Boyer was dead.

In the eerie silence that followed, the ghost of Bruce Donner gave the body he occupied back to its original host. The body crumpled to its knees. Bruce kept the mind, however, and watched the snake-thing free itself of its victim. A fissure opened in the floor. It glowed bright orange, like a crack in volcanic earth. The snake-thing flowed toward the gap, became one with the radiant magma, and disappeared. The rug sealed up, and after a puff of smoke vanished into the air, there was no sign of the fissure.

Seizing total control of his host, he picked up Wayne's body with unnatural strength, tossing it over his shoulder. Nobody saw him as he left Wayne's place, heading for the car parked two blocks away. He drove to a remote section of the woods and dumped Wayne's body there, knowing it would be found eventually. In the meantime, Hayley would wonder what had happened to her new writer.

That done, he headed home. Driving felt strange, being confined in a corporeal form that was, in turn, confined in a metallic one. As soon as he lay down in the man's bed, he let his host free. At least, he freed enough to let him function in society. But a part of the man Bruce kept locked away—his memory of his past and of Hayley Seagel.

In her dreams that night, Hayley was back in her own past, in Boston. She was watching a rehearsal of *By Blood or by Marriage.* No one on the stage seemed to notice that the floor was crawling with snakes. Hayley tried to tell Kelly and the others to be careful, but they ignored her.

"Bruce wrote a good play," someone said.

Hayley turned to see Humphrey Bogart at her side. He was dressed in a gray topcoat, his hat shadowing most of his face. Bogart was a black-and-white contrast to the bright colors Hayley saw around her, as if he'd been cut and pasted from an old movie clip.

"How do you know it's good?" she asked. "You're dead."

"So's everybody else," Bogart said, indicating the stage.

Hayley looked at the actors again. They moved about

the stage in slow motion, their words echoing as if spoken through a tunnel, their faces deathly pale.

"Except *him*," she heard Bogart say. "He was dead once, but he's back again. You better be careful of him, Miss Seagel."

Kelly was leaning down toward one of the snakes, a cobra . . . that had Bruce Donner's head.

Kelly screamed and backed away.

Everyone else on the stage began to laugh. Hayley turned to offer Bogart a questioning glance, but he was gone. Jack sat in his place, staring at Hayley. A black circle tinged with blood marked the center of his forehead.

Jack opened his mouth as if to speak, but the only sound that came out was a long, low whistling noise, like a kettle left on a low boil. Hayley could see the frustration in his eyes, feel the desperate grip of his hands on her upper arms.

"Jack, what are you trying to tell me?"

Kelly's scream drew her attention back to the stage. The Bruce-snake had grown as big as a man and was slithering up Kelly's body.

Hayley found a tv remote in her hand. She threw it with all her might, striking the snake. Its head flashed around; it hissed at her . . .

. . . and she bolted upright in her own bed. Across the room, there was a mark on the wall where the remote control had hit it. *The Maltese Falcon* flickered on the tv set.

She had fallen asleep watching a late movie. Slowly, shakily, she got up and retrieved the remote. Then she turned off the tv and headed for the bathroom, where she splashed cold water on her face to calm herself.

It had only been a dream, and yet she had a feeling the snakes had meaning. Something bad had happened, she was sure. But what, and to whom?

"Cut it out," she told herself, her voice unusually loud in the quiet of the house. "It's the dream talking. It's not real!"

When she went back to bed, the sensation of reptiles slithering around her made sleep long in coming.

The next morning, Wayne Boyer's landlady came knocking at his door in search of the month's rent. It was unusual that Wayne, always a good tenant, hadn't brought the payment down that morning. Rent was always collected on this date each month. Myra Stanley's thick-fingered hand knocked a little harder, causing the door to swing open. She frowned. Why had he left the door unlocked? Mr. Boyer was a very private person. He always locked his door, claiming he didn't want to be disturbed while working.

Slowly she entered the apartment, an illegal setup that had once been bedrooms for her four children. When they'd gone off and married, she and her husband, David, changed the rooms over to make extra income. They'd justified it to themselves by saying there was no other way to afford their property taxes.

Inside the small apartment, Myra was immediately struck by the smell of something burning. She turned back toward the staircase and yelled down:

"David! Come up here!"

Her husband, a stocky man with a ring of jet-black hair around a bald head, lumbered up the stairs a few minutes later. He made a face at the stench.

"Wonder why the smoke alarm didn't go off," he said.

The Stanleys walked through the apartment, but found nothing wrong until Myra noticed something on the rug behind the coffee table. She touched the spot gingerly, then drew back her hand in a flash.

"What's this slime?" she asked.

"Beats me," David said. He was beginning to feel uneasy. "Let's just get out of here. We can ask Mr. Boyer what happened when he comes home."

"You bet I'll ask him," Myra said.

The two went downstairs, not realizing they'd never see Wayne Boyer again.

6

Saturday night came more quickly than anyone anticipated. Hayley and Kate, in separate cars, were the first to arrive at the Athena. The manager, a man whose darkly handsome features belied his true age, greeted them warmly. Hayley's hand ached after he shook it, and she flexed her fingers all the way to the empty banquet room he'd set aside as their backstage area.

"Is this okay?" he asked. "There's a bathroom over there, and I've set up coffee and some hors d'oeuvres . . ."

"It's great," Kate said.

"You didn't have to go to all this trouble," Hayley said as she looked at the small spread he'd set out.

"It was my pleasure," the manager said. "You enjoy. I have to tend to my customers. The play begins at nine?"

"That's right."

"Just about an hour from now," Kate said, checking

her watch as the man left. "Everyone should be here in a few minutes."

Hayley sighed. "Well, I'll feel better when I've got us all lined up."

Andy was the first to arrive.

"Break a leg, dear," he said to Hayley as he kissed her cheek.

Andy was followed by Aidan, then Julianna and her husband, Jamie. Hayley was surprised to see their baby in Jamie's arms. She hoped Taylor would sleep through, and not disturb the restaurant patrons. But before she could say a word, Sean arrived.

"Where's Wayne?" Kate asked. "You two are always together."

Sean shrugged. "Beats me. I went to his apartment, but no one answered. The landlady told me she hasn't seen him in days, and he missed his last rent payment."

"That's strange," Hayley commented.

Andy snorted. "Probably too jealous to come watch Aidan's play."

Kate tossed a hand saying, "Oh, he'll show up."

Sean, gesturing to the table at the back of the room, said, "In the meantime, I'm going to check out those goodies."

Sean's actions seemed to draw everyone's attention to the spread of coffee and pastries for the first time. While they treated themselves, Hayley left the room and sought out the manager.

"We'll be ready shortly," she told him. "Just one more to come."

The manager smiled, then turned to help a newly arrived patron.

When Hayley returned to the banquet room, she was surprised to see everyone gathered in a cluster. Only Julianna stood apart, clutching Taylor as if to protect her from something. Hayley pushed through the group to find Aidan slumped over in a folding chair, head buried between his knees. Andy was kneeling beside him. The older man looked up at Hayley with concern in his bright blue eyes.

"Aidan, what's wrong?" Hayley asked, her voice pitched high with worry.

Aidan just moaned.

"It hit him all of a sudden," Jamie said. "He drank some coffee, and a few minutes later he was doubled over like this."

"What did you eat, Aidan?" Hayley asked.

"I don't think he can answer," Andy said. "Poor guy's in terrible shape."

Hayley looked around at the group.

"Is everyone else all right?"

A chorus of positives answered her.

"I think it was the coffee," Sean said. "Aidan's the only person to drink any. It made him sick really fast."

"I'll get the manager," Hana offered, hurrying toward the door. She was back in moments, the manager at her side, as Andy said, "Looks like food poisoning to me."

"That's impossible!" the manager cried. "We keep a strictly sanitary environment here!"

Hayley had been looking around the room. She spotted a partially empty coffee cup, retrieved it, and sniffed the remaining contents. She'd expected to detect sour milk, at the least, but the remaining drink smelled delicious. She smelled the pot—the coffee there had a warm, pleasant aroma.

"I don't know," she said. "Sean, was that all he had?"

"I'm pretty sure," Sean said. "He said the food looked good, but he was too nervous to eat." Aidan moaned again, wrapping his arms around his waist.

The manager took the cup.

"I'm certain nothing is wrong with my food," he said. "Or my coffee. Maybe it's just stage fright."

"I wouldn't call being doubled over in pain stage fright," Kate said.

"Something is definitely wrong with Aidan," Hayley stated. "We have to get him to a doctor. Since the rest of you have to perform in a few minutes, I'll take him myself."

"Then you'll miss the play," Jamie said. "I can take him."

"Jamie . . ." Julianna's voice showed her worry.

"It's okay, Julianna," Jamie said reassuringly. "I'll only be gone for a few minutes."

As much as Hayley wanted to go with Aidan, she knew she had a commitment to her other actors. She smiled gratefully at Jamie.

"Thanks so much," she said. "And don't worry, I'll keep an eye on Taylor while the play is on." Taking control of herself, she stated, "You'll take over Aidan's role tonight, Sean."

Sean nodded, his eyes solemn.

"Sorry, Aidan," he said, patting the other man on the shoulder.

Aidan didn't even look up.

With Andy's help, Jamie led Aidan out the back door of the restaurant. Hayley followed, watching until the men had eased Andy onto the seat. She glanced at her watch. It was already 8:45. She hurried back to her company and was pleased to see that they were all in costume.

"I'm lucky my two characters are never in any scenes together," Sean told Hayley.

"It'll be hectic," Hayley warned. "But I'm sure you'll do okay."

Sean grinned.

"You'll be amazed at how fast I can change costumes," he said.

At last it was nine o'clock. Hayley had assigned the job of introducing Jackal Mystery Productions to Kate, who explained the concept with such flair she had the audience smiling even before the play began.

At the edge of the restaurant, Hayley found herself sharing a table with Hana's brother, Yoshihide. They hadn't met before, so Hayley quietly introduced herself as the lights went down and she settled Taylor's babycarrier on an adjacent chair.

"Sorry I didn't say hello sooner," she whispered.

"I understand," Yoshi said. "Hana told me what happened. It's too bad."

Taylor began to fuss, making some patrons turn toward them. Hayley stuck a pacifier in the baby's mouth. She'd wanted to ask why they'd brought the kid, but she hadn't wanted to sound nasty. Besides, her major concern right now was the play itself.

No, her major concern was Aidan's well-being. Try as she might, she couldn't put him out of her mind. Throughout the performance, she barely heard the laughter and applause. Her mind was completely filled with thoughts of Aidan. If only Jamie would get back with some news! But the play was finished and there was still no sign of him.

Joyous applause told the actors that they'd done a fine job with their first play. Hayley looked around at the smiling faces and wished that Aidan was here to see them. Instead, he was stuck in some emergency room.

Hayley suddenly realized that someone was patting her on the back. She looked up at an elderly woman, who smiled and complimented her. Other people spoke to her, too. Hana, Andy, and the others congratulated each other, then the company moved into the banquet room.

Kate, who had sensed Hayley's distress all night, put an arm around her shoulders.

"He'll be fine," she said. "It's probably just a bug."

"But he looked terrible," Hayley said.

"And why isn't Jamie back yet?" Julianna added worriedly. The moment the play was over, she'd reclaimed Taylor from Hayley.

Sean came up to Hayley. He looked both hopeful and nervous.

"Did I do all right tonight?" he asked. "I know it was last minute, but . . ."

Hayley didn't remember Sean's performance at all, but she couldn't say that.

"You were fine, Sean," she said. "Everyone did a great job. Thanks for standing in for Aidan."

"I wonder how he is?" Sean asked. None of them could stay away from the topic.

Even Julianna chimed in. "My brother works in a lab," she said. "I could have him analyze the coffee."

"That's a great idea," Hayley said.

She went to retrieve the cup, but to her dismay, it was gone. So was the pot.

"Someone took it away," she said.

Andy put in his two cents' worth.

"Guilty conscience," he said. "The manager insisted nothing was wrong with the coffee, but he made damn certain we didn't have a chance to find out."

"Probably thought we'd sue him," Sean said.

Kate held up her hands.

"Now wait a minute," she said. "That's a nasty accusation. We can't go around treating our clients like this, or Jackal will be out of business before the summer is half over!"

"Kate's right," Hayley said. "Probably it was just an unfortunate incident. The important thing is . . ."

The door opened, and Jamie entered the room. Hayley fell silent.

"They're keeping him overnight," Jamie said. "He barely got through the hospital doors when he started vomiting bloody stuff."

"Oh!" Julianna cried, cuddling the baby closer to her as if to shield Taylor from floating squadrons of germs. She went to her husband, who put an arm around her.

"I've got to go see him," Hayley said. "Kate, let's square things with the manager."

She looked around the room.

"Thank you, everyone, for a great job," she said. "I'm sorry to have to run . . ."

"We understand," Hana said. "I hope Aidan is all right."

"Call me and let me know," Sean said. "I stay up pretty late, and I won't be able to sleep, anyway."

"Neither will I," Andy said.

Hayley nodded. While Kate gathered up their papers and everyone exchanged good nights, Hayley went to find the manager. There was a hint of disquiet in his expression. Although she wanted to blame someone for what had happened to Aidan, Hayley held herself in check. After all, even if it had been food poisoning, it was a terrible accident.

"I'm so sorry about your friend," the manager said. "I've made up these complimentary dinner coupons . . ."

Hayley shook her head.

"You don't have to do that," she said. "We're not blaming you. It was probably just a bug."

"Such a shame," the manager said. "But the play was wonderful. Four customers asked me when we plan to do it again. I'd like to book you for another two weekends."

Despite her worries, this brought a smile to Hayley's face.

"Thank you," she said. "Our manager, Kate Reising, handles that."

As if on cue, Kate appeared. She was delighted to hear that Jackal had additional bookings, and set up the dates with the manager.

"Great," she said when they finished, turning to Hayley. "Well! It's been an interesting night, hasn't it?" She patted Hayley on the shoulder. "Let's go to the hospital to check on Aidan."

"I hope he's all right," the manager interjected. "I have these dinner coupons, a little way to make up for what happened, but Ms. Seagel won't take them."

Kate had no such qualms. She slipped the bundle of envelopes into her briefcase and thanked the man. Then she led Hayley out to her car.

"I hope we can get in to see him," Hayley said as they drove away.

"It's kind of late," Kate said, "but at least we might be able to get some information."

But when they spoke to the hospital's triage nurse, it seemed they wouldn't even get that much. The nurse, a big woman with a long face and a dour expression, reminded Hayley of all the mean teachers she'd ever had in school. It took an effort to remind herself that she had a right to be here, and to be treated with respect.

"Listen," Hayley said in a firm voice. "Aidan McGilray is one of my employees."

"We've already notified his family," the nurse said.

Kate mumbled something that sounded like "Sounds like he's dead, for Chrissakes."

"Aidan was about to go on as a lead in our play," Hayley went on. "He became ill very suddenly. I feel responsible for him. Can't you at least tell us if he's okay?"

The nurse locked eyes with Hayley for a few moments.

Hayley felt as if she were being stared down, but she refused to budge. A simple answer was all she needed.

"All right," the nurse said. "I suppose it wouldn't hurt to release a little information. Mr. McGilray is going to be fine in a few days. We pumped his stomach."

Kate groaned and turned away.

"Then the poison is out of him?" Hayley asked.

"How do you know it was poison?" The triage nurse's eyes thinned.

"It seemed like food poisoning," Hayley said.

The nurse looked dubious, but before she could say anything more, the phone rang and she turned to answer it. Seeing she'd get no more information, Hayley turned away.

"What a bitch," Kate growled as they left.

"Aidan's going to be all right," Hayley said, to reassure herself as much as Kate. "Thank God. I was so worried when I saw him."

"Hayley," Kate said, "don't let this keep you up all night. Remember, we've got another performance tomorrow. Do you want me to take you back to the restaurant so you can get your car, or should we just go straight home?"

"I'd better get my car," Hayley said as Kate started up the engine.

Once they reached the restaurant's parking lot, Hayley quickly got into her car. She leaned out the window to talk to Kate.

"I don't think a nuclear attack could keep me up tonight," she said. "I'm exhausted. I'm almost tempted to cancel my piano lessons tomorrow so I can sleep in."

"But you won't," Kate said. "You like those kids too much. Just put all this out of your mind and get some rest, okay? You can straighten out things with Aidan in the morning."

Hayley took off for home, stifling a yawn. She carefully concentrated on the road ahead, telling herself it was only a twenty-minute drive.

A softly blinking light made her focus on a jogger running along the roadside. Her headlights were catching the reflective tape on his vest and flickering as his body moved up and down. She veered a little to avoid him, wondering why anyone would jog at night. She looked into her rearview mirror to check the jogger's position, but the road seemed deserted.

"You'd think he'd put reflective tape on the front, too," she mumbled.

When she looked again at the road ahead, she saw another jogger. Amazingly, this man was stark naked. As Hayley approached him, gazing wide-eyed, he stopped and turned toward her car. She could see all of him, right up to the grin on his face. He waved at her, smiling.

Then he ran out in front of her car. Hayley screamed, slamming on her brakes.

"Oh dear God," she moaned, turning off the engine. She hurried out of the car and ran to check on the man.

There was no one in the road. Heart pounding, Hayley crouched down to look under the car. Nothing but empty roadway.

"I know I saw someone!" she cried out.

She went all around the car, looked left and right, but if there had been a man, he was gone now. How could he have disappeared so fast?

Shaking, she got back into her car. Half of her debated going to the police, half of her said they'd think she was crazy.

I hit a nude man on the highway, but he vanished.

It was probably just a vision, brought on by exhaustion and tension. All she knew was that she wanted to get home as fast as possible. She drove much faster than usual, keeping her eyes firmly on the road ahead.

When she got home, Hayley went straight to bed. She was so worn out with fear that she fell asleep at once. But the night's trauma stayed in her mind, and brought back the dream. Jack and Kelly. Kelly held her black balloons, but three of them had burst and hung limply from her hand. Jack took a step forward.

"You have to listen to us, Hayley. You're in danger. Get away!"

Hayley's voice filled the void of her dream, bouncing off walls she couldn't see past the surrounding mist.

"Why am I in danger, Jack? Help me!"

"You know who he is," Jack said. *"He was supposed to be there that night!"*

"Who?"

But the dream faded away.

Hayley lay awake for a while, trying to make sense of it all. The dreams weren't exactly like the strange visions she'd had earlier in her life, but they meant something. Jack and Kelly were coming into her mind to tell her something important, and for some reason, they just couldn't.

Maybe someone had poisoned Aidan on purpose. Maybe the same person had taped the rat to her window. But who, and why?

She finally fell asleep with no answers.

7

When the ringing telephone woke her the next morning, Hayley practically leaped from the bed to catch it before the answering machine picked up. Perhaps it was news about Aidan. But as soon as she lifted the receiver, she heard a click, then the dial tone. Hayley looked through the archway at the kitchen clock to see it was only seven in the morning.

"Idiot," she growled.

Resigned to the fact that she was up earlier than she'd planned, she trodded into the kitchen to make herself a cup of hot cocoa. A few minutes later, she was relaxing on the roof deck, holding her crystal mouse, still wearing her nightgown and robe. The crickets were already singing to each other. Hayley had heard you could guess the day's temperature by counting their chirps—something to do with the number of chirps in fourteen seconds, then adding forty. She'd never been able to do it, but she guessed that the louder and faster the crickets rubbed their legs, the hotter the day was going to be. Even though there was a week left in May, and a month until summer, this day promised to be a sultry one.

She thought of Aidan, probably still asleep in the hospital. Would he feel better this morning? It worried her to think that whoever was bothering her had decided to turn against members of her company.

Hayley sighed and spoke aloud, with only a passing seagull to hear her.

"All right, Kate," she said, as if her friend were there. "I admit it. I like the guy. I care about him."

Now Wayne came into her mind, and she wondered what had happened to him. Strange that he hadn't shown up the same night that someone poisoned Aidan. She knew that Wayne didn't regard Aidan very highly. He seemed jealous that Aidan had written the first play Jackal was performing. Could he have poisoned his rival?

"That's ridiculous," she told herself. "Wayne Boyer isn't that sort of person."

She carried her empty cocoa cup down into the house, and dressed for her routine jog on the beach. The exercise helped clear her mind, and after finishing her household chores, she took off for the hospital. Aidan was sitting up in bed when she walked into his room. He was pale, but smiled when he saw Hayley.

"Hi," she said. "How're you feeling?"

She paused, wondering if she should kiss him on the cheek. That would be the way she'd greet any other friend in the hospital. But somehow she felt a little strange. The sight of him in that bed, his hair all corkscrews and his eyes shining in the overhead lights, made her heart flutter. He looked so . . . cute. There was no other word for it.

Stupid, she thought, *you're acting like a fifteen-year-old!*

She busied herself looking for a place to sit down. She dragged a chair over to the bed and sat.

"Better than last night," Aidan replied.

There was an awkward beat, then they both started talking at once. They both laughed, then Aidan held out a hand, giving her the floor.

"I'm so sorry about what happened," Hayley said.

"It wasn't your fault," Aidan said.

Hayley gazed into his eyes. Such nice eyes ... "But you're okay now, right?" There was hope in her voice.

Aidan seemed to understand her need for reassurance, because he took her hand and squeezed it. She felt her heart skip a beat and fought down a sense of giddiness.

"Much better," he said. "Whatever was in me, it's out now. In fact, I'm starting to feel hungry. All I got for breakfast was Jell-O."

"Jell-O for breakfast?" Hayley said with a laugh.

"Clear liquids," Aidan said. "It's part of the deal."

Without giving herself time to think about it, Hayley spoke quickly.

"Then I'll make it up to you," she said. "Maybe you can come by my house one night for dinner."

There, it was done. She had never thought she'd be cooking for someone after Jack, but pushed aside the little voice that was trying to tell her this was improper.

"That'd be great," Aidan said, his smile broadening.

God, he's got a gorgeous smile, Hayley thought.

"So, how did it go last night?" Aidan asked.

"Fine," Hayley said. "Sean took over your part."

Aidan nodded his approval.

"Sean's got a lot of talent," he said.

"Well, let's hope he won't have to understudy for you again," Hayley said. "I picked you for that role because you're just right." She went on, "I'm so glad you're going to be okay. Did the doctor tell you what he thinks happened?"

"They sent samples down to the lab," Aidan said. "But I haven't heard anything. Actually, the only thing I want to hear is that I'm being released."

A nurse walked in just then, and Hayley turned away as she took Aidan's temperature and blood pressure. She wasn't squeamish; she just felt that she was invading Aidan's privacy.

"They woke me up at least three times last night to do that," Aidan said ruefully when the nurse left. "Whoever said hospitals are a place to rest never stayed in one."

Hayley laughed, grateful to see that Aidan's spirits were up. It seemed that last night's incident was only minor, after all. Aidan was going to be fine.

There was a knock on the door and a short, stocky young woman entered. She had a round, freckled face and curly brown hair.

Aidan smiled and said hi, then introduced the women, saying, "Hayley, this is my sister, Jan."

Hayley and Jan shook hands. "You've both got the same eyes," Hayley said.

"Nice to meet you," Jan said. "Aidan was telling me about you the other night."

"Oh?" He was already talking to his family about her?

"Only good things," Jan insisted. She shook her head at her brother. "How'd you manage to get into this situation?"

"Lousy coffee." Aidan shrugged. "I don't know. I just doubled over in pain last night. Did you talk to Billy?"

He looked at Hayley. "That's my older brother. He's supposed to be checking on Lady, my puppy."

"I couldn't get him on the phone," Jan said. "Didn't he say something about camping?"

Aidan grimaced. "That's right. I forgot. What do I do about Lady now?"

"Don't look at me," Jan said. "You know my allergies can't take being near any cat or dog."

"I can check up on her, if you'd like," Hayley volunteered. "In fact, if you're going to be here awhile, I'd be happy to take her to my house."

"You'd do that?" Aidan's smile seemed particularly bright. "That'd be great. I wouldn't ask, except that she's only a baby."

"No problem," Hayley said with a wave of her hand. "I like dogs. She'll love running around the beach."

Aidan pointed to the closet.

"My keys are in my jeans. The house key is blue."

Jan found the keys, took the blue one off the ring, and handed it to Hayley. Aidan wrote down directions to his house.

"I really appreciate this," he said.

Hayley smiled, then gathered up her things. "Well, I'm off. Don't worry, Aidan."

"Just so Lady wants to come back to me," Aidan said. "She might like the beach *too* much."

Hayley left without kissing him good-bye, even though part of her wanted to. She felt strange about showing him affection in front of a family member. She did care about him, but she wasn't sure she wanted anyone to think it was deeper than that.

"He can help you, Hayley."

Hayley jumped, turning around although she knew she was alone in the elevator. The voice had been loud and clear . . .

Jack's voice.

"Jack?" she whispered.

The elevator doors slid open to reveal a young man

pushing a gurney bearing a sheet-covered body. Hayley froze.

"Excuse me, miss," the young man said.

She blinked and realized there was no body. The gurney carried nothing but a pile of neatly folded and stacked sheets, along with a few boxes of bandages.

Hayley hurried off the elevator on the ground floor. She waited for Jack to speak to her again, wished for it, but heard nothing at all. As she walked to her car, she thought again of the dream she'd had. Maybe the voice had only been the vestiges of that, appearing because she was tired. She wasn't surprised that she'd dreamed of Jack and Kelly last night. After all, watching a good friend become very ill was enough to give anyone nightmares. The only thing Hayley couldn't understand was why it was that particular dream. Was the message Jack and Kelly were trying to relate connected with last night's incident?

When she arrived at Aidan's place, she let herself in to the sound of frantic yelping. Hayley went quickly to the kitchen, where she released Lady from her pen. The dog jumped all over her, wiggly body language saying:

I don't know why you came, but I'll be eternally grateful to you for setting me free.

Lady punctuated it by peeing on the floor. It was just a few drops, quickly cleaned up. Hayley got the puppy some food and water, which calmed her down. She cleaned up the pen, which Lady had soiled during the night. When the puppy finished eating, she gathered up its toys and put a leash on it. To her surprise, Lady sat quietly during the whole drive to Hayley's place. When she opened the door, the dog bounded toward the sand with happy barks.

"Don't get lost," Hayley said. The house was isolated enough that she wasn't worried about losing the puppy.

She went inside the house, hanging both her keys and Aidan's on the hook mounted on the wall just inside her kitchen door. Then she pulled open the curtains over the sliding doors, keeping an eye on Lady as she played back her phone messages. There were two, one from Kate reminding her that she was driving to the restaurant that night, and one from Wayne. The man sounded strange.

"I'm sorry I missed the play last night," he said. His voice was shaking, cracked, as if he'd been crying. "I'm very sorry. I was running a little late, but then I realized you people didn't want me there. It wasn't my play, after all. I don't understand, Hayley. I was only going to be a little late. Why didn't you wait for me?"

The last sentence sent chills through Hayley, chills that quickly hardened to anger. What did Wayne mean by that? She flipped through her file on Jackal and looked up his number, planning to confront him. She let the phone ring twenty times, but there was no answer. Slowly she hung up. She closed her eyes and tried to catch her breath.

Could it be Wayne who'd been terrorizing her? The man was a writer, and might easily have heard about Bruce Donner. After all, Bruce had won a Tony award and had been somewhat famous. Hayley vowed to demand some answers from Wayne as soon as possible. In the meantime, though, there was just too much work to do.

8

Bruce had a vague memory of being fettered by his own corporeal form, but that life seemed to belong to someone else. It hadn't been a healthy body, he remembered. Liver ruined by too much alcohol, scars from fights, a punctured ear drum. This body, however, was young and healthy, but he still felt penned up.

It wouldn't stay healthy for long. He would let it live long enough to destroy everyone, Hayley last of all. Then he would make the body's host commit suicide. He'd leave a note that the police could use to trace him back to Boston; the connection would be made, and all would be right with the world.

He wouldn't hurt Hayley until nearly the end. He'd just scare her a little, like he'd done with the rat. The thought of that rodent hanging on the window made him laugh. It was a laugh issued through a borrowed larynx, but it had become familiar to him over the past days. He'd first heard it on the plane ride from Boston, when he'd laughed with glee at his triumphant possession of this individual. The man had once been a big fan of his. Too bad he'd never know the great role he was playing in a Bruce Donner production.

He looked around the small apartment, taking in the minimal furniture. Everything looked green to him, as if he were looking through special night-vision goggles. Everything smelled like cinnamon or vinegar. He heard an animal making noise from another room. He didn't know if it was a dog or a cat. Might even be a bird. He hadn't mastered the nuances of hearing. He was able to make out voices just fine, but they all sounded strange. He remembered yelling through moving fan blades as a kid, the way the blades sliced the words to pieces. Everyone sounded like that.

Except on the telephone. He liked the way Hayley's voice sounded on the telephone. He'd thought about calling her last night, just to say something about that Irish jerk. He would survive the poison he'd been given, but that was all right. Bruce had a much more interesting demise planned for Aidan McGilray. Anyone who dared to love the woman who had scorned him deserved pain.

He knew the host's routine, and realized it was time to give back the body. The man had a job to go to. Bruce, too, had work to do, work that didn't require a physical form. He had to study his next victim, find out what terrified her, so that he'd be ready when it was time to strike again.

9

Jackal's second performance went off without a hitch. Content, Hayley slept late the following morning. It wasn't until Lady's excited barking that she pulled herself from bed to jog and walk the dog. The day progressed without incident, her piano students all excited to meet Lady. Hayley went to sleep that night thinking of Aidan, wishing he could have seen how much better the second performance of his play had gone, planning to visit him again the next day, if he wasn't ready to be discharged.

Aidan occupied her conscious mind, but as sleep dragged her deeper into its vortex, it was Jack she saw. Kelly stood with him as before. Hayley realized Kelly held seven black balloons, including the broken ones. Seven. The number of people in Jackal Mystery Productions.

Hayley reached toward Jack, but he backed away from her.

"I can't," he said. "I can't!"

He seemed ready to cry, as if he were terribly frustrated.

"Can't what?" Hayley asked. "Jack, what are you trying to tell me?"

Jack only shook his head. "He'll destroy us."

"Who?" Hayley asked. Her voice sounded clear, not like a dream voice. She felt aware of everything around her, as if she were awake.

But she couldn't be awake. Jack and Kelly didn't exist in the waking world.

"You know who he is," Jack said. "He was supposed to be there that day."

"Jack, who are you talking about? Please, tell me. Is it Wayne?"

Jack only shook his head, looking sorry.

"Be very careful, Hayley."

"He's getting closer," said Kelly.

"Who?"

The sound of her own voice woke Hayley. She lay wide-eyed for a long time, trying to understand. If only Jack and Kelly could tell her exactly what they meant! She thought the "who" in the dream must be Bruce Donner, but why couldn't they say so? What power did Bruce hold over them?

Although this dream had been less frightening and bloody than the ones she'd had before, it was more disturbing. How the hell could she fight a ghost?

"God help me," she whispered, clutching at her pillow. "What do you want with me, Bruce?"

She closed her eyes and listened to her heart pounding with fear. Gradually, it slowed and she fell asleep again. Her next dream was more pleasant, of a day she'd spent on Jack's sailboat. Jack became Aidan in the dream, but it was Jack's voice that said:

"Be strong, Hayley. Be strong."

When she woke up, she felt different. She was still wary, but her terror had turned to angry determination. What the hell right did Bruce have to ruin her life now?

"You won't!" she yelled out loud to her empty bedroom. "Just because you fucked up doesn't mean you'll drag me down. This is *my* company. Mine! Do you hear me? *I'm not going to let you stop me!*"

Although there was nothing to answer her but house noises, she had a feeling that somewhere Bruce was laughing at her, mocking her. Let him laugh. She'd be stronger than he was, no matter what!

Hayley was the first person Aidan thought of when he was told he could leave the hospital Monday morning. He fished through his pockets to find the paper on which he'd written her phone number. But a feeling that he might be pushing things if he asked her for a ride home made him reconsider. There was something about Hayley that told him she was shy about starting a new relationship. Was it right for him to move so quickly? From the moment he'd first met her, during auditions, he knew she was someone he wanted to get to know better. But maybe he should move slowly, back off a little.

"I probably shouldn't have let her take the puppy, either," he told himself as he dressed.

He hadn't planned for her to take Lady, it had just happened. Well, the beach was a great place for a puppy to play if she had to be away from her master.

Instead of Hayley, Aidan phoned his brother, who had returned from his weekend camping trip. When Billy reached the hospital, Aidan saw that his brother was sunburned and walked with a slight limp.

"What happened to you?" Aidan asked.

"Too much hiking," Billy said.

Discharge papers taken care of, the two left together.

"So, how do you feel now?" Billy asked as they rode down in the elevator.

"Better than last night, for damn sure," Aidan said.

"Jan said it was food poisoning," Billy said. "Is that what they told you?"

Aidan shrugged.

"This is just a small community hospital," Aidan said, "and on Sunday, the lab only does emergency work. If there's anything to be found in the tests, I won't know until tomorrow, at the earliest. I'm just grateful I can go home now. Hospitals suck."

"Spoken like a true Beavis and Butthead fan," Billy said. "I bet the real reason they let you go was so they wouldn't have to look at you."

Aidan laughed, registering the sarcasm in Billy's voice. His brother looked enough like him to be his twin, although Billy was four inches taller and a little heavier.

They climbed into Billy's pickup.

"Jan says you've got a girlfriend," Billy commented as they drove toward Aidan's home.

"Guess so."

"Hey, come on," Billy pressed, "you can't keep her a secret forever. Who is she?"

"She heads up this new theater group I'm involved with," Aidan said. "I like her, but I don't think she's my girl."

"Not yet," Billy said, teasing.

"Actually," Aidan admitted, "I'm worried that I might be moving a little too fast."

"At your age, fast is the only way to go when it comes to romance."

"At my age?" Aidan said. "You're older than me, Billy."

"And I'm married with kids. Which reminds me, Michael's just crazy about that new video game you sent over. He says it's the best thing you ever designed."

"Mike's my best critic," Aidan said with a nod.

Billy stopped for a red light. "So what's her name?"

"Who?"

"Who!" Billy cried, rolling his eyes.

"Hayley Seagel," Aidan replied. "Didn't Jan remember that?"

"You know Jan," Billy said. "A little daft, a lot forgetful."

"A lot the tired mother of five kids," Aidan said in his sister's defense.

They'd reached Aidan's house. The first thing Aidan noticed upon entering the kitchen was the clean kennel. He'd never expected Hayley to do that, and it only strengthened his feelings for her. Anyone who'd clean up puppy mess was someone worth knowing better.

Billy stayed for only a short while, then had to get back to his store, Billy's Bait'N'Tackle. As soon as he was gone, Aidan called Hayley, wanting to thank her for looking after Lady.

When he got her answering machine, he decided to drive over there. After all, he felt one hundred percent better now, and was sure seeing Hayley would do him good.

As Hayley was working on her lesson plans for that day's students, a soft woof made her turn. Lady gazed up at her. As soon as they made eye contact, the dog dropped down on her front legs, her hindquarters up in

the air. The signal that she wanted to play was one
Hayley had seen many other dogs perform.

"All right, then," she said. "Let's go for a run. All this
paperwork is getting to me."

She opened the sliding doors and the dog followed her
out to the sand. Hayley stopped to lock the doors, and it
occured to her that she'd never had to lock up in the day-
time before.

An hour later, when they were nearly home after a vig-
orous run, Lady suddenly stopped short, cocked her head,
and seemed to be listening intently to something Hayley
couldn't hear. Then, with excited yaps, the puppy tore
away, running toward the house. Hayley followed
quickly. When she came around the front of the house,
she saw someone bent toward the window, peering into
her living room behind a cupped hand. Lady darted forward, barking steadily.

"What are you doing there?" she demanded.

To her relief, it was Aidan. As he approached, looking
worried, Hayley realized she must look half terrified.

"What's wrong, Hayley?" he asked. "When no one answered the door, I was just checking to see if Lady was
in there. I'm sorry if I . . ."

"It's okay," Hayley insisted.

Lady tore in and out between Aidan's legs, until he
bent down and scooped her into his arms.

"You should have called first," Hayley said as they entered the house together.

"I got your answering machine," Aidan said. "So I
thought I'd come over instead."

"Well, I'm glad to see you," Hayley said. "You look
okay."

He looked better than okay, but she wasn't going to let
herself think about that too much. She led him into the
kitchen.

"Do you want some iced tea?" Hayley asked.

"Sure."

As she made up two tall glasses of tea, Hayley thought she might tell him about the call from Wayne, but decided against it. A stay in the hospital was enough for Aidan to deal with.

"Sorry I scared you," Aidan said. "You didn't really think you'd have a prowler at ten in the morning, did you?"

Hayley shrugged. "What brings you here? I wasn't expecting you to come for Lady for a day or two. And what about your work?"

"I called in sick," Aidan said.

Hayley nodded, gazing at him. Then she grinned. "You work at home," she said.

"I called myself," Aidan explained.

Now Hayley laughed out loud.

"You've got a great laugh," Aidan said. "Your whole face lights up. Makes you even prettier."

Hayley bit her lip and turned away from him. The flattery made her a little uncomfortable. For all she knew she was blushing, God help her.

Some woman of the nineties you are, Hayley. Maybe the 1890s!

"Hayley, are you nervous?"

She turned back to him, her eyes full of questions.

"About what?"

Was she that obvious? She had dated only rarely in recent years, didn't recall the little nuances, the way to do it smoothly. Was she making a fool of herself?

"About seeing someone nosing around your front door," Aidan explained.

"Oh!"

He wasn't thinking about her shy act at all.

God, he must think I'm a complete airhead.

"Well, it's just that . . ." She sighed deeply. Aidan seemed to know something was wrong, and his concern brought the truth out of her. It felt right to tell him of her worries.

"It's just that I'm concerned because of the things that have been happening," she said. "And Wayne called me last night. He sounded very strange."

She told Aidan about the call, but left out her feelings about Wayne's final question. That was too painful, too private to share with a man she hardly knew.

"Sounds like he tied on one," Aidan said. "Forgive me if I sound like I'm bragging, but I think he was jealous of me."

"To be honest, so do I. But I'm still going to confront him. I don't like the way he stood us up two nights in a row. I don't have much tolerance for whiny drunks."

Not anymore. Not since Bruce.

"Do what you think is right," Aidan said. He glanced at Lady, who had found a beetle to chase. "You know, it might not be a bad idea to get a dog yourself."

Hayley laughed again.

"Like Lady?" she asked. "That dog would go belly up for the worst criminal in New York."

"No, more of a watchdog type," Aidan said. "Rottweilers can be big mushes for their families, but they scare strangers half to death. Maybe you could check the shelters . . ."

"No thanks" Hayley said. "I'm just too busy to care for a dog."

"Oh!" Aidan cried, as if a lightbulb had gone on inside his head. "I forgot to thank you for cleaning up after Lady. I never expected you to do that."

"Any job worth doing is worth finishing," Hayley said. "And it was no trouble. Lady's a great dog. We had a lot of fun together, didn't we, girl?"

Lady wagged her tail.

Aidan stood up. "Well, I've got to get back to work. Thanks again, Hayley."

He bent and kissed her gently on the lips. She wasn't exactly surprised by the gesture, but it caught her off guard enough to render her speechless for a few seconds. Before she recovered, he was already at the front door. She got up quickly and went after him.

"Any time," she said. "Lady just loves the beach here."

"You've given me an idea," Aidan said. "I'm going to make one of the levels of my newest video game take place on a beach, with a dog for an ally."

"A magical dog," Hayley said, "and maybe you could work in a lighthouse like the one at Montauk Point. The lighthouse could be a gateway to another dimension."

Aidan grinned. "You're good. Do you play video games?"

"Not really," Hayley said. "They lost their novelty for me after Ms. Pac-Man."

"Then you don't know what you're missing," Aidan said. "Remind me to take you to an arcade with my nephews."

"No thanks," Hayley said. "I can handle dogs, but I'm not sure I could deal with space invaders."

Aidan walked away, laughing. He stopped at his car and called back:

"If you think you can handle a dog," he said, "I know where you can get a nice one. Think about it, Hayley."

"I will!" she promised.

Hayley watched him drove off, a deep sigh bringing her shoulders up and down. She waited for guilt feelings about Jack to settle in, but they never came.

That, she decided, might be a sign that it really was time to move on.

But there was also her daily life to tend to, and she'd noticed when she was getting out the pitcher of iced tea that her refrigerator was nearly empty. Gathering up her keys and handbag, she left the house to do some shopping. She had plenty of time before her first student would arrive.

There was a restaurant across the street from the grocery store. Although it was usually Kate who handled the bookings, Hayley decided she'd see if she could also get them a job.

The owner of the restaurant was a delightful grayhaired woman who absolutely loved Hayley's idea. The two of them chatted for quite a long time, and the woman even treated Hayley to lunch. To her delight, she booked an entire weekend in August before she had dessert.

After she finished her shopping, a glance at the clock on her dashboard told Hayley she'd been out longer than she'd planned. Her first student of the day would be at her house in just half an hour. It would only take a few minutes to get home. So far, the day had gone very well.

Sometimes, Hayley told herself, things actually went right.

10

The next rehearsal was scheduled for Hayley's house. This time, she didn't protest when Aidan volunteered to come early to help rearrange the furniture. They made small talk, and Hayley was pleased to find she felt very comfortable with him. The shyness she'd felt during their first meetings seemed to have left her, and she was glad of it. She didn't even feel bothered when he noticed a picture of Jack and her that sat on a small wicker stand. She didn't wait for him to ask questions.

"That was Jack Langley," she said. "He meant a lot to me, a long time ago."

"Looks like a nice guy," Aidan said easily.

He didn't seem jealous at all, and that pleased Hayley. Still, she took the picture from him.

"He was," she said simply. "But he died."

"I'm sorry, Hayley," Aidan said.

He seemed to sense that she wanted to reveal nothing more and changed the subject at once.

"Have you heard from Wayne yet?"

"No, except for that strange call," Hayley said, setting the picture back in its place. "I tried getting back to him, but no one answers. If he doesn't show up tonight, maybe I'll go over there to talk to him."

"Sean could check on him," Aidan suggested. "He lives close by."

The doorbell rang and Kate arrived, followed close behind by Sean.

"We were just talking about you," Hayley said to the young man.

His eyebrows went up. "Oh?"

"Wondering if you've seen Wayne," Aidan put in. "Hayley hasn't been able to get in touch with him."

Kate made an annoyed face as she set down her purse.

"Neither have I," she said. "If he's going to fink out on us, I need to know. Because if he isn't, I've got to figure his pay into our budget. And I don't want to play cat and mouse games, chasing him!"

Sean ran a hand through his hair, looking apologetic.

"I went to his apartment," he said. "No one answered the door. His landlady said he's been gone for several days, and since the rent is due, she thinks he skipped out on her."

Hayley considered this. "He might have. I know writers go for stretches where they don't make much money. Maybe he's between checks, and broke."

"Then why forfeit the chance for a paycheck?" Kate asked. "I know we don't have much to give, but it would have helped. If you ask me, he decided he didn't want to work with Jackal after all, and didn't have the decency to tell us!"

Hayley laughed. "This from the man's biggest fan? You were so enthusiastic about him!"

"I was until I met him," Kate said. "Now I think he's a snob."

"Oh, I don't think so," Sean said. "He's a wonderful author. They get temperamental, you know."

Leaving them to talk about Wayne, Hayley went into the kitchen to make a pot of coffee. Wayne being missing was really starting to worry her.

"Hayley, I need to talk to you," she heard Kate say as her friend came to stand beside her, getting a fresh coffee filter from the package as Hayley opened the coffee can.

"Is it about Wayne?" Hayley asked.

Kate shook her head.

"No, it's something else," she said. "I had another dream about the Shadow Man."

"Oh, no," Hayley said. Was this mysterious Shadow Man going to haunt Kate the way Jack and Kelly were appearing to her? But the Shadow Man was only a dream. She didn't want to think the evil was engulfing her best friend's life, too.

"Hayley, it was terrible!" Kate said. "It seemed so real! He was nothing but a dark shadow. No face, no features at all. But he spoke to me. He said he'd come back again, just like before."

Hayley concentrated on making the coffee for a few moments, collecting her thoughts.

"But it was just a dream," she said gently, "like last time."

"I don't know," Kate replied. "I threw a glass of wine at him. It went right through him and hit the wall. When I woke up, the glass was gone, but the stain was on the wall!"

"Sometimes people act out during nightmares," Hayley

pointed out. "You must have had a glass of wine next to your bed . . ."

Kate shook her head. "There was no glass on the floor. But there's something more important. I don't have any red wine at all in the house. I had company for dinner the other night and realized I was out of it."

Hayley gazed at her friend. She thought of the visions she'd had recently of things that weren't there.

"Kate . . ."

Before she could speak, Sean poked his head in the door and said:

"Everyone's here. Ready to start?"

"You bet," Kate said. She looked at Hayley. "Anything's better than thinking about that dream!"

Hayley followed her into the living room. She still wanted to talk about the wine stain, but there was no time now. Julianna had arrived, toting baby Taylor as usual. Hayley thought for a moment that Julianna was the most overprotective mother she'd ever seen. Then she noticed Hana and smiled at the pretty young woman. Hana returned a slight smile of her own.

"You look tired," Hayley said.

"Bad night," Hana replied. "I had a strange dream." She frowned. "I don't want to talk about it."

Hayley looked over at Kate, who gave her head a slight shake. The significance of Hana also having a strange dream wasn't lost on her.

"So Boyer hasn't shown up yet?" Andy asked.

"Forget about him," Aidan said. "I think he's a lost cause."

"I agree," Julianna said. "Let's forget about him."

"That's right," Andy said. "Aidan's play was a hit the other night. Too bad you missed it, kid. Applause for your own work can be intoxicating."

Hayley opened her briefcase and took out her own copy of the script.

"Then let's work on it tonight," she said. "You know we're booked for a new restaurant next Saturday."

"Oh!" Kate said. "God, I've been so preoccupied I forgot about some exciting news I got today."

"Tell us," Sean said eagerly.

Everyone turned to Kate.

"Well, I hear a critic from *Newsday* might stop in," she said. "He'd heard about the play, and he's going to come see it."

"Wonderful!" Julianna cried. "Will he be taking pictures?"

"I don't know," Kate said. "I don't even know when he'll show up."

"Then we'll have to practice extra hard," Hayley said. "We want the play to be as flawless as possible so we get a good review. There were a few points I jotted down . . ."

The rest of the night passed quickly, a mix of laughter and some arguments over delivery of lines. Julianna had to interrupt everyone to feed Taylor a bottle, but she recited her lines as she held the baby. Andy amused everyone with a quick tune on the piano, giving Hayley an idea to work it into another production. Nobody mentioned Wayne Boyer again.

At the end of the evening, they all said good-bye until only Hayley, Kate, and Aidan were left. Kate, thinking Hayley might like to be alone with Aidan, quickly gathered up her paperwork. Hayley stopped her.

"Kate, what about the wine?" she whispered.

Kate managed a smile. "You know, maybe I did have a *little* wine in the house. Just enough for a nightcap. I suppose I forgot."

"You really think so?" Hayley asked. "You aren't just saying that so I don't worry, are you?"

"When have you ever known me to be less than straight-forward?" Kate asked. "Forget about it, Hayley. Just concentrate on that cute guy over there."

"Kate!" Hayley whispered forcefully.

Kate opened the door, looking back over her shoulder to give Hayley an encouraging smile. Hayley widened her eyes at her, telling Kate silently that she was making too much of this too soon.

She looked around the room.

"Well, I guess I can move the furniture back in the morning."

"Why?" Aidan asked. "I'll help you."

"I just thought . . . you might be tired."

Hayley wanted him to stay, but she didn't want to push things.

"I'm just fine," Aidan said. "C'mon, you take the other end of the couch."

In a short time, the furniture was all replaced. Now Aidan started fidgeting with knicknacks. Hayley laughed.

"You don't have to do *that*," she said.

"I'm delaying," Aidan admitted. "I hate to leave you alone, Hayley."

He came closer to her, raised his hands as if to hug her, then dropped them slowly. Hayley rested her hands on his arms.

"I'll be okay," she said. "I've been living alone here for five years. Believe me, if I hear anything unusual, I'll call the police."

She sensed that Aidan wanted her to invite him to stay, but she wasn't ready for that yet. As much as she was attracted to him, as much as she cared about him, she just wasn't ready to sleep with him. When it came to intimacy, her heart still belonged to Jack.

"I'm very tired," she said.

"Uh-huh," Aidan said absently, looking back at the opened sliding doors. The half-moon looked grayish through the mesh screen.

"Aidan . . ."

"Oh!" He seemed to come awake suddenly. "I—I guess I'd better be going. Are you sure you don't want me to stay?"

God, do I ever want you to stay!

Hayley ignored her thoughts.

"No," she said. "I refuse to live in fear."

"But you'll lock the doors and windows?"

"Do you want to walk around the house and watch me do it?"

It took Aidan a few moments to realize she was kidding. He managed a laugh.

"Sorry, I guess I'm being over-protective. Is that sexist?"

"It's kind," Hayley said. "I appreciate your concern."

He stared at her for a moment. "I *am* concerned about you, Hayley. You . . ."

He paused, as if fishing for the right words. Hayley watched him carefully.

"You're very special," Aidan said. "Hayley . . ."

As if there were no right words for the moment, he stopped talking and bent down to kiss her. She backed away a step, a gesture that surprised even her.

"Aidan, please," she said. "I'm just not ready for this. Please . . ."

She felt awkward, foolish. She wanted him so much, and yet she couldn't bring herself to tell him so. Was it because they'd been talking about Jack earlier that evening?

"I'm sorry," she stammered.

"It's okay," Aidan said. "Really. It's okay."

Hayley yawned involuntarily. Aidan took this as a sign he was staying too long. He bent down and kissed her on the cheek, a friendly gesture she accepted without protest.

"I'll go," Aidan said. "If you're sure . . ."

"I'm sure." Hayley said firmly.

She stood in the doorway as he walked out to his car. Her heart began to beat faster, and she felt a cry rising from her: *Stay! I want you with me tonight.*

She couldn't do it.

He stopped halfway up the driveway, stalling even further, and turned.

"You really should get a dog."

"We already discussed that."

"A Rottweiler or a German shepherd."

"I'll think about it, Aidan," Hayley said, closing the subject. "Goodnight, Aidan. See you next rehearsal."

"Goodnight, Hayley."

She shut the door.

And wanted to open it again and call him back inside. But she wouldn't do that. She told herself it was just that she didn't feel right, with Jack's memory still strong.

But how long would Jack's memory remain this strong? Five years had gone by! How long did it take to get over someone you loved so much?

Did you ever get over him?

And if you couldn't, what difference would it make if you committed yourself to someone new?

"Lots of difference," Hayley said out loud as she walked to her living room. "It wouldn't be fair to Aidan."

She felt confused, part of her drawn back to the memory of Jack, part of her reaching out for a new love. What was she going to do?

She sighed and looked around the living room.

"I know what I'm going to do," she said out loud. "Right now, I'm going to lock up my house."

True to her word, she went around the house closing and locking doors and windows. It was only a small bungalow, and the job was quickly completed. She checked the coffeemaker to make sure she'd unplugged it, then headed for her room. A half hour later she was asleep and dreaming.

It might have been Fourth of July, because fireworks were going off in the sky. Hayley was standing near a picnic table resplendent with summer foods like corn on the cob and fried chicken. She couldn't tell if this was Montauk or Boston. Jack was standing at the barbecue, his back to Hayley. Kelly was tying black balloons to the trees.

"That one's broken," Hayley said.

Kelly turned to her. "He wants to break you."

"Bruce does."

Kelly looked frightened suddenly, as if she'd said too much. She turned away from Hayley. In her dream, Hayley took a determined step forward.

"Why are you afraid of him?" she asked. "Why can't you say his name?"

Jack stabbed at something on the barbecue, then turned slowly.

"You already know who he is," he said. "He was supposed to be there that day."

Hayley saw the bloody gunshot wound in the middle of his forehead, the dead rat hanging from his barbecue fork.

She started to scream . . .

. . . woke up . . .

. . . and found herself looking into a pair of eyes.

For a split second, her mind didn't register what she saw. Then Bruce smiled and said:

"I didn't want to leave you alone tonight."

Hayley screamed frantically, jumping from the bed.

"Get away from me!" she cried. "Get away! You're *dead*!"

She ran from the room, stumbled across the living room and bumped her hip hard against the telephone stand. The vibrations made the shelf above rattle, knocking over the crystal mouse. With a gasp, Hayley managed to catch it mid-air. As if it were magical, Jack's gift helped her calm down. Hayley took a few deep breaths and turned to look at the opened door to her bedroom.

Bruce had not been there. She'd been having a terrible nightmare.

No, Bruce was powerful, strengthened by evil. He was appearing to her the way Jack had appeared once, not through dreams but in reality. He was trying to scare her to death.

To death.

"No!" Hayley cried out.

How dare he? How dare he invade her home and her life?

"Go back to hell, Bruce Donner!" she screamed.

She didn't think about what she was doing, just let her anger drive her into the bedroom. She'd fight him!

He wasn't there.

"Where are you?" she demanded, even as her sixth sense told her that he was gone.

If he'd really been there at all.

She saw her wild reflection in her mirror. She looked like some cavewoman, mad with terror, eyes wide, hair standing on end, grimacing broadly.

Then Bruce was gazing out at her from the glass, laughing silently.

"Leave me *alone*!" Hayley shouted.

She picked up a small bronze statue and threw it, shattering the mirror.

For a few moments, she stood there gasping, staring at the empty frame with its jagged edges.

"I'll stop you," she said, forcing out each word. "I'll find a way!"

Just then, she heard a loud crash outside her bedroom window, followed by the frantic sound of a dog yelping. Pulling on her robe, she hurried to investigate. She didn't bother bringing a weapon. There was no weapon that could fight a ghost.

The summer night was quiet, with only the lulling sound of the ocean to fill her pounding ears. She guessed that the sound had come from behind the staircase that led to the rooftop deck. Some animal might have tried to climb it, and fallen . . .

But she knew there was no natural explanation when she found the little dog crumpled beneath the staircase. Slats of light shining through the empty spaces between the steps illuminated its tragic form. Hayley let her weak knees give way, and she knelt beside the animal. She reached for it with shaking hands. Her finger found a deep indentation, still gushing blood, still warm. And then she saw its ear, a tiny ear with a little nick in it. Lady's ear.

She burst into tears of rage. Somehow, someone had murdered Lady and dumped the body at her house.

Aidan's response to Hayley's near-hysterical call was as immediate as possible. Unable to understand her, he got in his car and drove to Montauk. When he arrived, she was sitting on the couch, her eyes red and her face blotched. She'd been crying. A police officer was standing next to her, notebook in hand. Aidan gave him a quick look, then sat down beside Hayley. She didn't resist when he put his arm around her and pulled her close to him in a protective embrace.

"Hayley, what's this all about?" he asked.

"It's Lady!" Hayley said. "Someone's killed Lady!"

Aidan shook his head in wonder.

"That's crazy," he said. "Lady's in her kennel at my house, safe and sound."

"N—no, she isn't," Hayley gasped.

"Someone shot a puppy and left it here," the cop told him. "You want to take a look?"

"I will," Aidan said, "but I know for a fact it isn't my dog."

Behind the house, he knelt beside the dead puppy, shaking his head.

"It sure looks like her," he said softly. "Someone went to a lot of trouble to get a setter. Poor little thing."

"He saw us together," Hayley said from a few feet away. She didn't want to go near it. "He went to your house and took her!"

"Impossible," Aidan said. "She was in her kennel when I left, sound asleep."

"Are you sure?"

"I checked on her before I left."

He saw the concerned look on Hayley's face and reinforced that.

"She's fine, Hayley," he said. He looked at the cop. "What are you going to do about this?"

"I'll have the body taken away as evidence," was the reply, "and I'll suggest that a detective be assigned to this case. Stalking is a crime. Fortunately, we don't get much of it here in Montauk. But we do take care of our own."

He smiled at Hayley, but she didn't return the smile. Then he turned to Aidan.

"Can you stay with her?"

"I'm not going anywhere."

The cop called for help in handling the puppy. Hayley stayed inside the house as the body was removed. Aidan sat beside her, holding her in his arms.

"I thought it was Lady," she said.

"I know."

Tears began to stream down Hayley's cheeks.

"Who is doing this to me?" she whispered.

"The police will catch him," Aidan promised.

"But when? When?"

Aidan's strong hand took hold of her chin and turned her to face him.

"Listen to me," he said. "No matter what happens, I'm here for you. I'm going to stay by your side and help you through this, okay?"

"Oh, Aidan . . ." Hayley whispered.

And suddenly they were kissing. There were no feelings of guilt, no thoughts of Jack. Only the warmth and goodness of the moment, a strong feeling of attraction that had been churning inside of Hayley from the moment she first saw Aidan. She held him as tightly as she could, as if he could protect her from everything bad.

He found the buckle of her belt and started to work at it. The old uncomfortable feelings started to rush back, and though Hayley tried to fight them, she couldn't. She knew they were a sign things were moving too fast for her. She took hold of his wrist.

"Not yet," she said. "Aidan, please, just hold me. All I want now is for you to hold me."

"All right," Aidan whispered. "It's okay, Hayley."

Right now, holding her would be enough. They didn't say anything more. And as if Aidan was a sort of guardian angel, Hayley slept in his arms without dreaming.

11

The sun was just coming up when Hayley woke up in her bed the following morning. She turned over and felt a twinge of disappointment to see she was alone. She didn't remember going to bed. Where was Aidan now? Quietly she got up and went out to the living room.

The wicker couch was empty, but it was too small for him, anyway. A slight ruffling of the vertical blinds led her to the sliding doors, and she found him sound asleep on a recliner. He'd found the down comforter she stored in the top of a closet. A mess of windblown hair and two thickly-lashed, closed eyes were all she could see of him. She smiled warmly. Last night, in her distraught state-of-mind, she had been very vulnerable. If he'd wanted to, he could have taken advantage of that. Other men might have done so. But Aidan had chosen to respect her, sleeping out here instead of climbing into her bed.

Not that she would have been angry to find him there. In spite of her protests, he would have been welcome. But the idea that he had enough respect for her to wait made her feel all the more affection for him.

He looked so comfortable that she decided not to wake him. Instead, she went inside and made herself a cup of hot chocolate, then quietly carried it up to the roof to watch the sunrise. It was beautiful over the Atlantic, jewels of color dancing on the waves. It was so quiet now, almost a dreamland. Hayley remembered that dawn had been one of Jack's favorite moments when he'd come down here with her.

"Is it okay, Jack?" she whispered. "I hope it's okay. He seems like a nice guy."

Jack didn't answer her.

She saw a lone jogger trotting along the shoreline, a dog at his side, and was reminded of the poor little dead dog. Her moment of contentment seemed to crash with the speed of the sunlight suddenly filling the sky. She had a sick feeling that there was blood on the sand below the stairs. She wanted to clean it up right away, to get rid of any trace of that heinous act.

Hayley didn't mean to make a lot of noise as she hurried down the stairs, but she was so intent on her purpose that her feet seemed to stamp out her feelings. She was bending over under the stairs, staring down at the sand, when Aidan spoke her name. Startled, she stood up quickly.

Aidan's hand shot out, keeping her from banging her head.

"Whoa!" he cried. "You'll knock yourself out that way. What're you doing?"

"Looking for blood. I don't want blood near my house."

"I'm sure all that was cleaned up and taken as evidence," Aidan said. "Say, do I smell cocoa?"

"It's just hot chocolate," Hayley said, grateful for the diversion. "Come on in. I'll make you some."

She filled the pan with milk again, then opened her cupboards.

"I don't have any eggs left," she said. "There's a muffin in the bread box. I'm having cereal myself."

"Cereal's fine," Aidan said.

Over breakfast, they talked about what had happened.

"It's amazing how sick some people can be," Aidan said. "Some poor family is missing that little dog today."

"I had a dog that ran away when I was a kid," Hayley recalled. "We did everything we could to find her, but it was as if she'd disappeared off the face of the earth. You never realize how big the world is until you lose something in it."

Aidan finished his hot chocolate before speaking again.

"Well, if someone's missing that puppy," he said, "they'll contact the police, or the animal shelters. The news will get back to them, rotten as it is."

Hayley thought about this. Then she said:

"Maybe nobody's looking for the puppy at all. Maybe someone bought the dog for just this purpose."

"Hayley, she looked like a pedigree," Aidan pointed out. "A dog like that could cost four hundred dollars. Who'd bother?"

"But maybe it wasn't from a breeder," she said. "Maybe it was adopted from a shelter! It might only have looked like a purebred, in the darkness."

"Where are your Yellow Pages?"

"Huh?"

"We've got some shelters to visit," Aidan said. "We need to look them up."

"You'd come with me?" Hayley asked. "But I don't want to keep you from your work."

"I sent in two proposals yesterday," Aidan said. "I can't do much until they call me. So I'm free this morning."

A half-hour later, armed with a list of shelters, they set off. The nearest one was thirty miles away. This early in the morning, they were the first visitors. The woman was very friendly, inviting them to sit down, but when she learned they weren't there to adopt, her manner grew a bit cool. No, she didn't remember anyone adopting an Irish setter recently.

Hayley and Aidan got the same stories from the next two shelters. Growing increasingly frustrated, Hayley was about to give up. Maybe the dog had come from a breeder, after all. Maybe there would be no clues.

"Just one more," Aidan said. "It's only about three miles from here."

"I don't want to waste your gas on a wild goose chase," Hayley said.

"Don't worry about it,' Aidan said. "It's my fifteen cents a mile, not yours."

The elderly gentleman at the next shelter told them that yes, someone had adopted a female Setter mix about a week earlier. But adoptions were confidential, he was sorry to say. He couldn't help them.

Hayley put her on most pitiful expression. It was easy to start weeping—all she had to do was think about that poor little dog she'd found under her stairs.

"Please," she said. "We lost our poor Lady recently, and we're so afraid someone adopted her by accident. I know you can't break a confidence, but could you just tell us one thing? Did the dog have a nick in her ear, near her head?"

The old man's eyes widened, and he nodded slowly. That fine a detail could only come from someone who knew the dog. Finally he turned to a file cabinet. It took him some time to dig up the papers, which he turned over to Hayley without further question.

"Sure hope it helps," he said. "That fella seemed real taken with that dog. I hope you can get her back."

"Oh my God," Hayley whispered as she read the form.

"What's wrong, Hayley?" Aidan asked quietly.

Hayley gave her head a slight shake and handed the paper back to the shelter worker.

"Funny thing," she said. Hopefully only Aidan could tell her smile was forced. "A friend of mine came and got the dog. He must be holding her for me. Thanks so much."

With that, she turned and hurried from the place, Aidan in pursuit. In the car, she took a deep breath and said, "Wayne Boyer's name was on the paper."

"What?"

"He was the person who adopted that dog," Hayley went on. "He killed it."

Aidan whistled softly as he started the engine.

"I knew the guy was a curmudgeon," he said, "but I didn't think he'd do something like this. It doesn't make sense."

"None of this makes sense," Hayley said. "Aidan, can we drive to his apartment? Maybe the landlady can tell us something."

On the way, Hayley tried to fight the feeling that something was wrong with her conclusion. Even Aidan had agreed it didn't make sense. Why would Wayne Boyer harbor such resentment toward a woman she barely knew, who ran a small theater company? And if he'd known Bruce Donner well enough to have inside information on his death, how come she'd never heard of him before?

Hayley felt a chill rush through her. Bruce Donner. Had Bruce really come back . . .

. . . the way Ricky had come back; the way Jack had come to her?

"What are you thinking about?" Aidan wanted to know.

Hayley wrapped her arms around herself. "Just nervous, I guess. I can't pinpoint my feelings, but I think we're heading in the wrong direction."

"But you saw Wayne's signature on that paper," Aidan said. "It seems pretty concrete to me, even if we don't understand it. Here's Wayne's place. Let's see what the landlady can tell us."

But Myra Stanley couldn't tell them a thing.

"Only thing I know is, he left all his things behind," she said as she led them up to his apartment. "Only things missing are his wallet and keys."

She pushed open the door and they entered his apartment.

"Have a look for yourselves," Myra said. "If there's any hint you can give me, let me know. I can't do without that rent money."

She shut the door and left them alone. They walked through the small apartment together, taking in the minimal furniture, the *Writer's Digest*s scattered over the coffee table and the state-of-the-art computer tucked under the eaves.

"He must have spent all his money on that," Hayley said. "He certainly didn't spent in on furniture."

"Or on family," Aidan said. "There aren't any pictures around, except for that group shot next to the telephone."

Hayley picked up the photo and studied it. Wayne, flushed and probably drunk, was staring with a bright-eyed smile at the camera. His arm was around the neck of a pretty young woman. Another couple shared the restaurant booth. Pictures of old trains decorated the wall behind them.

"Something looks familiar about this place," Hayley said. "But I can't remember where it is."

With a strong feeling this was a clue, she looked at the back of the picture with no results. Setting it down again, she went to look for the kitchen.

"I tried already," Aidan said. "He used a microwave and a hotplate. It's an illegal apartment."

Hayley nodded. "I get it. That's why Mrs. Stanley hasn't filed a missing persons report. She doesn't want to get caught."

"Well, we've got to tell the police," Aidan said. "We don't need to get the Stanleys in trouble. They're probably just trying to make ends meet. But we can tell the cops about the puppy's adoption papers."

When they arrived at their local precinct, they were introduced to a police officer named Pat Alan. Pat was an attractive woman whose brown hair was twisted up beneath her cap. The pockets and buttons and paraphernalia of her uniform only enhanced her figure. Hayley was immediately struck by the fact she seemed at least ten years younger than either Hayley or Aidan. Hayley told Pat all about the dog, and the form signed by Wayne Boyer.

"*The* Wayne Boyer?"

"You've heard of him?"

Hayley remembered how excited Kate had been to hear that Wayne was joining Jackal Mystery Productions.

"I read all his books," Pat says. "But there's a prob-

lem. He just couldn't have been the one to sign that paper. Not if it was done recently."

Hayley and Aidan exchanged frowns.

"What do you mean?" Hayley asked.

"He's dead," Pat said simply. "His body was found by
a scout troop taking a hike through the Pine Barrens. It
seems he died of a heart attack."

"A heart attack," Aidan repeated.

Hayley could hardly believe it.

"How long had he been dead?"

"Several days, maybe a week," Pat said.

"And it doesn't seem like foul play to you?" said
Aidan.

Pat shook her head. "That's not what the coroner's report indicates. Probably the guy was out hiking when he
collapsed. There was one thing, though . . ."

"What?" Hayley asked.

"There were a few marks on him that appeared to be
snake bites," Pat replied. "At first the coroner thought
that he might have been attacked by someone's loose pet
snake. The scare might have caused his heart attack."

Aidan asked if they'd found the snake, but Pat's reply
was negative.

"The game warden conducted a search of the area,"
she said. "We thought someone might have tired of an
animal that got too big to handle, and dumped it in the
woods. But nothing was found."

She shrugged. "I'm sorry I can't help about the puppy."

Hayley felt frustrated as she and Aidan left the building. They'd reached a dead end. She'd hoped Wayne was
the guilty party. As much as it seemed to be Bruce, it
would be easier to take if a human were responsible.

"I just don't see how it could have happened," she said

as they drove home. "If Wayne is dead, he couldn't have put that puppy under my stairs."

"Then who did?" Aidan pondered. "Who went to such great trouble to find a dog just like my Lady, knowing it would upset you?"

Hayley nodded. "How many dogs are there with nicks just exactly at the base of the left ear?"

Aidan let out a laugh.

"This isn't very funny," Hayley growled.

"He made a mistake," Aidan said. "Lady's nick isn't on her left ear. It's on her *right* ear."

"Oh," Hayley replied. She rubbed her eyes and turned to look out the window, going into deep thought. She didn't say a word for a long time as she tried to piece together what she knew so far. She kept remembering the picture she'd found in Wayne's apartment. Why had it looked so familiar?

At last she came up with the answer. It was a pub in Boston, a place where she'd gone sometimes with her theater company. Wayne Boyer had also been there.

"Maybe he knew Bruce," she said out loud.

"What?"

"I think Wayne Boyer knew Bruce Donner," she said.

"Who's that?"

Hayley realized she'd never said a word about Bruce to Aidan. Maybe now was the time.

"I told you Jack meant a lot to me," she began. "That wasn't quite right. He meant more to me than anyone I've ever known. I really loved him."

She went on to tell Aidan about Boston and her work there, Bruce Donner and his drinking problems, and about Bruce's plans to move everyone to New York.

They were nearly to her house when she reached the hardest part of the story.

"It was a sort of anniversary," Hayley said. "While I was out running errands, my good friend Kelly Palmer came to my apartment to help Jack set up a party. It was supposed to be a surprise. But they . . . Bruce came and . . ."

She had to stop herself. She didn't want to start crying, but it was so hard to talk about that day. The sides of her neck started to hurt. Hayley realized she was gritting her teeth.

"Take your time," Aidan coaxed.

Hayley took a deep breath.

"I'm all right," she said. She rubbed her eyes, drying them.

"Bruce came to the apartment, too," she said. "I'm not sure what happened, because there were no witnesses. But he . . . he shot both of them in the head."

"Oh, damn," Aidan whispered.

"I think they died instantly," Hayley said. "When I found them, Bruce was still there. He said it was a surprise for me. I just ran . . . I don't remember much after that. The police questioned me for hours, but I couldn't tell them anything. I suppose I could have noticed Bruce had some problems if I'd taken the time to look. If I hadn't been so busy . . ."

Aidan reached across the seat and squeezed her hand.

"Don't bother with 'ifs'," he said. "It's a waste of time."

"I never really got any answers myself," Hayley went on. "Bruce killed himself in the jail cell."

She paused, unable to relate how she'd found Bruce hanging in his cell. Eventually, she continued. "I had a pretty bad time of it after that. It's the reason I came to Montauk. I wanted to relax in a familiar, safe place, far from Boston. Kate helped me get settled, start teaching piano. In fact, she was the one who sold me on the idea of starting Jackal Mystery Productions."

She sighed deeply, staring at the road ahead.

"It seems all my current problems started with this company," she said. "Someone doesn't want me to go on with it, and he's trying some pretty mean ways to stop me. I thought it was Wayne."

"Whoever he is, I hope he's wasting his time," Aidan said. "You aren't going to let him win, are you?"

"Hell, no," Hayley said, "but it's very scary, Aidan."

They'd reached Hayley's house. Aidan parked in the driveway and they both got out.

"Would you . . . walk me inside?"

She hated to play the damsel in distress. But she wasn't stupid, either. Broad daylight aside, she wanted to make sure she was really alone before Aidan left.

"I had planned to," Aidan said. "I could spend the day, if you want."

Hayley shook her head.

"I'll be fine," she said. "Besides, what would Lady do? She's just a baby, you know. You shouldn't leave her."

"Then you could come back to my place."

Hayley fished out her keys and unlocked the front door.

"No, that's okay," Hayley said. "I appreciate the offer, Aidan. But I've got a full afternoon of piano students. And I'm not going to let anyone drive me from the home that's been in my family since I was a little girl."

Aidan smiled broadly.

"Maybe you should take up kung fu with me," he said. "They teach a good self-defense course for beginners."

Hayley smiled back.

"I'll think about it."

Aidan put his hands on her shoulders, and without another word kissed her. His kiss was warm and sweet and Hayley welcomed it. Her arms found their way around him, and she moved into the warmth of his embrace. For just those few moments, there was only Aidan, and nothing else in the world mattered.

12

Killing the puppy had been easy. It had been so trusting, just as the man at the shelter had trusted he was going to be a good owner. Those people were so desperate for adoptive parents they probably would have given him a dozen puppies to do with as he wished. But even a dozen puppies couldn't match the thrill of one human life.

It was time to kill again.

He'd used Wayne Boyer's name to confuse Hayley, but the discovery of the writer's body changed things. He had to make certain Hayley understood his message. He had to kill in a way that some would think an accident, but Hayley would understand.

There was to be a rehearsal at the dancer's house. He'd learned that while in possession of his host's body. Tonight, he would choose his next victim.

* * *

That night, at rehearsal, Hayley tried to push aside thoughts of Wayne Boyer and the dead puppy, in order to concentrate on her work. But every once in a while, the image of that poor little animal would rise to her conscious mind. She pushed at it, driving it away. Wayne wouldn't be gotten rid of so easily, though. She hated to think that he had suffered. What did a snake bite feel like? Had it really been a snake bite?

"Here have a soda," Kate said. "You look like you could use scotch, but this is all we've got."

"I can't stop thinking about what's happened," Hayley said. "Poor Wayne! Nobody deserves to die in such a lonely way."

"A snake bite," Kate said, shaking her head. "I can hardly believe it. People are so irresponsible."

Hayley didn't tell her she thought that no snake was involved in Wayne's death. She changed the subject, forcing herself to give her all to that night's performance.

"Everyone's here but Hana," she said. "That's the third time she's been late since we've started."

"I'll have to talk to her about it," Kate said. "This is getting out of hand. If Hana can't handle this, we'll have to let her go."

"I hate to do that," Hayley said. "It's just one more problem for us."

Now Aidan joined them.

"You both look troubled," he said.

"Hana's late," Hayley told him.

"That's not it," Aidan said. "You're still thinking about Wayne. It wasn't your fault, Hayley. You had nothing to do with it."

Hayley sighed. "It's just that Jackal has had so much bad luck."

Aidan held up a hand, then went to the raincoat he'd hung up next to Julianna's staircase. It was pouring out-

side that night, and lightning flashed even as they prepared for rehearsal. He pulled out a bunch of folded
pages, then went back to the women.

"Here's something else to think about," he said, unfolding it. "It could be our next play."

"Aidan!" Hayley said in surprise. "You didn't say a
word about it!"

She took it from him and scanned the top page.

" 'Die, Team, Die!'," she read the title. "A college
football mystery! What a riot!"

"This is great," Kate said.

Sean, Andy and Julianna, attracted by their enthusi-
asm, came closer.

"We have a new play to rehearse?" Sean asked.

Hayley nodded eagerly. "We can start tonight. Aidan,
why didn't you say anything?"

"I was still working on it," he said. "I don't like talking about things until they're done. But you seemed to
need a diversion."

"Besides, we can't do the same play forever," Kate
said. "We have to diversify if we're going to grow as a
company."

Andy leaned closer as if to see the script better.

"What kind of roles are there?" he asked. "Football
players, I presume."

"Only one," Aidan said. "That would be Sean. It takes
place the day before the big homecoming game."

He went on to tell them the plot. Encouraged by their
laughter, he decided to describe the characters.

"I wrote this one with all of us in mind," he said. He
looked from Hayley to Kate. "I hope you don't mind that
I've written down some casting suggestions."

"Not at all," Hayley said, reading his list. "These are
great. Andy's just right for the coach. Kate's the school
principal and Julianna's Sean's mother."

Julianna laughed. "I don't look old enough to be his mother. Hope you're going to put some gray in my hair."

"Don't worry," Andy said, "we'll make you a real old fogey, like me."

"You're not an old fogey," Sean said.

"What about Hana?" Kate asked.

"This is great," Hayley said. "Hana plays a cheerleader. But she's a little off-the-wall. She uses nunchakus instead of pom-poms!"

"Perfect!" Andy said.

Julianna looked out the window at the storm.

"I wonder what's holding her up?" she asked. "She's never been this late before."

"You do have to talk to her about that," Andy said. "She's holding up the rest of us."

"Oh, it's just a few minutes," said Sean. "And she works as hard, maybe harder, than anyone."

Hayley looked at her watch. They'd been here nearly forty minutes. Maybe Kate was right. Maybe it was time to give Hana an ultimatum. Still, she had to take a chance that there was a good explanation. In the meantime, they'd waited long enough.

"Let's get started," she said.

"I'm sorry I didn't make copies," Aidan said. "But I just printed that out at the last minute, before I came here."

"We can start next time," Hayley said. "In the meantime, let's perfect our current play."

Hana glanced at the clock on her dashboard and saw to her chagrin that she was even later than usual. Damn this storm! It was bad enough a fight with her aunt and uncle had held her up, but the hazardous road conditions were really slowing her.

Far ahead, a bolt of lightning struck the horizon, as if to tell her it didn't care about her problems.

As she drove, peering hard through the rain, she thought about the argument she'd had with her family. Uncle Leo and Aunt Mariko had brought her, and her older brother Yoshihide, from Japan when their parents were killed in an earthquake. Hana had been five at the time. She remembered little of her days in Japan and had grown up as American as any natural-born citizen.

Without much help from her guardians, she thought. In spite of being successful manufacturers of business machines, in spite of having lived in America even longer than Hana and Yoshi, they were stuck in their old, traditional ways. Hana's upbringing had been very strict. Neither Uncle Leo nor Aunt Mariko approved of her joining a theater group. They considered American theater to be distasteful, and sometimes even immoral.

"But this is just a small group," Hana had argued with them that night. "We do mystery plays for fun. It isn't like I'm going to be dancing naked, for God's sake."

Mariko had shuddered. The idea of a woman's body being exposed in front of strangers was anathema to her.

"If you want to work in theater," Leo said, "perhaps you could join a Japanese troupe."

"Find one and I'll join it," Hana had said, her voice just slightly edged with sarcasm. She'd been punished enough as a child to know that Leo would tolerate no disrespect.

Yoshihide tried to come to her defense. At thirty-one, he was seven years her senior. He stood a half head taller than Leo, but still found his uncle formidable.

"These dinner theater groups are very popular," he said. "You see ads for them all the time in the newspaper. But Hana's right, it's all in fun. It won't occupy very much of her time."

Leo's eyes thinned. "As long as it doesn't interfere with her work at Musashi Enterprises."

Driving her car along the highway, Hana thought of his words, and the response she'd had to bite back. She wished something *would* interfere with her work at Musashi. All her life, she'd been pushed toward working for the family company. She took on the job out of obligation. After all, Leo and Mariko had done so much for her. In spite of being strict, they'd also been loving. But *having* to work for a company and *wanting* to work there were two different concepts. Yoshi had said that the theater group wouldn't occupy much of her time. If she had her way, it would occupy all her time.

"Someday," she said to herself, "I've got to stand up to them and tell Uncle Leo I don't want to work for Musashi Enterprises."

Someday soon, but not today, or tomorrow.

A sign indicated that her exit was coming up. Checking her mirrors to be sure the way was clear, Hana noticed a pair of headlights very close to her rear bumper. She took a quick look back over her shoulder. The road was virtually empty in the storm. Why was that person tailgating her?

She moved carefully to the next lane. The other car followed, then moved forward and bumped her car. Hana tried to speed up, but the car kept with her. She tried to reach the exit, but when the car hit her again it threw her out of control. With a screech, Hana's car spun crazily, hitting the divider, bouncing back, then turning until it was facing the wrong direction. Hana's breath caught in her throat as the other car turned around itself and came roaring back, brights glaring in the rain. It slammed her car hard, sending the vehicle in a mad zigzag toward the side of the road.

Too terrified to even scream, Hana did her best to

bring the car under control. Yoshi had taught her what to do in a skid, but to her horror she realized she had forgotten. Should she turn with a skid, or out of it? What the hell was she supposed to do?

The car careened off the road and onto the grass, where, thankfully, it came to a stop. The torrential rain had turned the dirt to mud, offering no traction as Hana tried desperately to free herself. No matter how hard she worked, the tires only dug in deeper.

She looked out at the road. The rain had subsided quite a bit, and she couldn't see any sign of the car that had hit her. Why the hell would anyone do such a thing, she wondered? Some drunken idiot, she guessed. Where were the cops when you needed them?

Well, she supposed she'd just have to sit here until another car came along. Hana fumbled for her emergency flashers, then sat rubbing her arms in an effort to calm herself down. Her legs were shaking so hard that her knees were actually knocking. It seemed she could hear the pounding of her heart.

"Hurry, hurry," she whispered, wishing a police car would appear.

She wouldn't let herself think that she might be sitting there for a long time. This far out on the island, the roads were lightly traveled, especially on a weeknight. How soon would Hayley and the others miss her? Would they call her home? As much as she needed help, she almost wished they wouldn't. Uncle Leo would never let her live this down. He would tell her it was a sign that she should have listened to him.

After what seemed an eternity, but was actually only fifteen minutes by her dashboard clock, Hana had calmed down completely. It was a horrible experience, but it was over. Even the rain had let up. She tried to remember what she'd passed on the road. There had been a diner a little ways back. Was it near enough to walk?

Then she heard a car engine and felt relief. At last there would be someone to help her. In spite of all she'd been taught about strangers, she didn't care to whom the car belonged. At this point, anyone who could get her out of this muddy prison would do.

She opened her door and got out. Holding up her white purse in the hopes it would catch the car's headlights, she began to wave it.

A moment later, she realized the car was on the wrong side of the road.

He was back.

"Oh, shit," Hana mumbled, throwing her purse aside.

There was no point in hiding in her car. He'd only find a way to break the windows. And she couldn't run. Every step made her sink deeper into the mud. There was only one place to hide.

Hana dropped to the ground and scrambled under her car. Seconds later, the other car pulled up nearby. Hana held her breath and watched in terror as the door opened and two boots appeared. They looked familiar, but she couldn't place them. It wasn't until the driver stood up and got out that she caught a glimpse of his face.

Wayne Boyer.

What was he doing here? Hana almost called out to him. After all, Wayne was a member of Jackal Mystery Productions. He was a friend of sorts—he couldn't have been the person who ran her off the road.

He swaggered toward her car, obviously drunk. He looked angry and mean. She couldn't begin to imagine why he'd want to hurt her, but maybe the alcohol had twisted his reasoning. Distraught with fear, she didn't even consider the fact that the dark and the rain should have made it impossible for him to know who she was.

He walked toward the back of the car. What the hell was he doing?

Just be quiet. Just wait. Just wait. Maybe he'll go away . . .

The mud beneath her was chilly. Smells of oil and gasoline made her want to gag, but she covered her mouth to help filter them.

Oh, God, please go away. I'm not here, okay? I ran off into the woods. Go away and I'll get in my car and get out of here . . .

He pushed on the trunk, making the car rock. Hana squeezed her eyes shut.

I'll drive home, I promise, Uncle Leo, I'll drive home and I won't come back to the group, I'll drive home if you go away!

The car rocked more violently now, hitting her back again and again.

He knew she was under here.

Go away, go away, go away, go away!

The rocking stopped. Wide-eyed, Hana watched the pair of legs walk away from the car. Maybe she should get out and reason with him. After all, he was an intelligent man. Whatever had happened to him to make him do this was not her fault. Maybe she could make him see that!

She took a deep breath for courage and started to crawl out from under the car. The sensation of something stroking her back made her stop. She felt gentle pressure moving down her back, massaging her. A soothing touch, but how. . . ?

Struggling, she turned her small frame to look up at the underbody of her car.

A hand was reaching toward her, fingers outstretched. Hana screamed.

The hand shot forward, grabbing her as she tried to

scramble out from under the car. With unnatural power, it held her fast as she desperately tried to get away.

She screamed. Her mind, trying to her rational, told her that Wayne had opened the hood and was reaching down past the engine and carburator.

But she could see Wayne standing near his own car, twenty feet away.

She grabbed the hand, trying to push it off her. Her eyes blinked in shock as she looked up.

The arm ended just above the elbow, melting into the chassis.

Oh, no, this is crazy, this isn't real.

"Go away!" she screamed.

Another hand appeared, oozing through the metal, reaching down, down.

The two phantom hands grabbed her throat and began to squeeze. Hana struggled as hard as she could, trying to use techniques she'd learned in karate to get out of this chokehold. But her position made it difficult, almost impossible. Her sight began to dim, until the twists of metal over her head faded away.

Her very last thought was of police sirens.

You're too late, she thought, falling into darkness.

13

The next few days were busy ones. Hayley attended Wayne's funeral, gazing through dark sunglasses at familiar and unfamiliar faces, wondering if anyone could answer her questions about his death. The somber mood increased her worry about Hana, whom she hadn't been able to contact. No one answered the phone at the Musashi house, not even a machine. By the time the weekend came, Hayley was hoping Hana would tell her everything the night of the play.

While the restaurant patrons enjoyed their dinners and waited for the show, Hayley worked her way through the crowded office that the company was using as a dressing room, looking for the young woman. Kate was helping Andy with a bow tie, Julianna was pinning up her hair, Sean was reading his lines to himself.

"Has anyone seen Hana?"

"She's always late," Julianna pointed out. "Can you zip me?"

Hayley stopped to slide the zipper up the back of Julianna's tight red dress. With veiled hat and high heels, she looked the part of the "Woman of Mystery." No one in the audience would believe she had a baby. When Hayley saw Aidan nearly trip over Taylor's carrier, she made a mental note to talk to Julianna about the baby. Having her around all the time was beginning to be a real problem. Right now, though, she was more concerned about Hana.

Julianna was right, of course. Hana *was* often late. She seemed to have a lot on her mind. Hayley was willing to help, but she also thought that personal problems should be left behind during work. She could use herself as an example. No one saw her whining about the terrible things that had been happening. She had shed tears for Wayne, had attended his funeral, but she knew that it was time to move on. There was work to do. The old phrase "the show must go on" might have grown trite with use, but it was still true.

"Well, it worries me," she said. "She missed the last rehearsal and hasn't been heard from since. What if something happened to her?"

"What if she's just unreliable?" Kate asked. "The least she could have done is to call us! There'd better be a damned good explanation, Hayley, or we're going to have to let her go. I know you don't like that idea . . ."

Hayley smiled a little. It was hard for her to be tough on people. But maybe Kate was right. Hana's chronic lateness and failure to show up was having a negative effect on the company. And they already had enough problems!

Still, she wished Hana would walk through the door. Aidan was pulling on a dark jacket for his role as a mobster. He noticed the worried expression on Hayley's face as she looked at the door. He came to her and gave her a brief, reassuring hug.

"What is it?" he asked quietly, leading her away from the others.

"Hana isn't here yet," Hayley said. "She's never been this late before. I'm really worried now."

She looked up into Aidan's eyes.

"What if something happened?" she asked softly. "What if the same person who tried to poison you is trying to sabotage tonight's performance, too?"

"You could try calling Hana's home," Aidan suggested.

"I already tried," Hayley said. "But I suppose it wouldn't hurt to do it again."

She picked up her notebook containing the cast's phone numbers and carried it out to the pay phone in the hall. After feeding quarters into the machine, she dialed. Once more, the phone rang without anyone picking up.

"No one's home," she said.

Aidan, who could see that her concern had grown even deeper, gave her arms a little rub.

"It'll be okay," he said. "You can call again in a little while, if she's still not here."

Kate approached.

"We go on in fifteen minutes," she said. "Where the hell is Hana?"

Hayley explained the situation. Kate, thinking quickly, said:

"You can take over her role, Hayley."

"But she's so young!" Hayley said. "I couldn't play that part!"

Kate's eyes thinned.

"We are not a pair of decrepit old biddies," she said evenly. "You can do it. She's only got ten lines, and I know that you've got this play memorized as well as any of us."

"Why can't you do her?" Hayley said. She didn't do much acting and usually felt uncomfortable performing.

"Because I have to do the German accent," Kate said. "Remember, that's why you picked me to be the psychiatrist. Besides, it's too big a role for me to take on another part."

Hayley couldn't argue with her logic. "Okay, then. But I'll need help with the waitress costume. Hana is smaller than me."

Hayley was able to squeeze into the skirt, which had an elastic waist. But there was no way she could get into the top.

"Five minutes," Sean said.

"What are we going to do?" Hayley demanded.

It seemed she was going to have problems at every performance, with or without outside influence.

Andy came to the rescue, pulling a tuxedo shirt from the costume box and handing it to Hayley.

"It'll do," he said. "Any of you ladies have a ribbon for a bow tie?"

Julianna found one, and Hayley tied it on. The restaurant manager poked his head in, and was given the okay to announce the start of the show.

"Break a leg," Andy whispered to Hayley.

"The way things are going," Hayley whispered back, "I probably will."

An hour later, they were congratulating each other in the little room. Hayley felt flushed, overwhelmed by the applause she'd received. She'd forgotten how much fun acting could be, once she relaxed.

"You should join us out there more often," Andy said.

"Yeah, you were great," Sean added.

Hayley shook her head. "Hana would have done much better."

"I'm not so sure about that," Julianna said. "You're very talented, Hayley. Producer, director, and actress."

"A triple threat," Andy said with a grin.

Aidan took Hayley by the arm and steered her from the group. He gave her a quick kiss of congratulations.

"Good job," he said.

Hayley was beginning to feel silly from all the praise. She was about to make some offhand remark when she noticed officer Pat Alan talking to the restaurant manager. Something congealed in the pit of her stomach. She didn't need to hear what they were saying to know something was wrong—and that it had to do with her company.

"Hana," she whispered.

"What's that, my dear?" Andy inquired.

Hayley ignored him, hurrying over to the cop.

"This police officer wants to talk to you, Ms. Seagel," said the manager. He stepped away to give them privacy.

"I understand that Hana Musashi is a member of your theater company?" Pat asked.

"Oh God . . ."

Pat regarded her steadily, waiting for an answer. Hayley found her voice.

"She's one of my actors," Hayley confirmed. "Why? What's happened to her?"

"She was hurt very badly in a car accident," Pat replied. "I need to ask you some questions."

"Accident?" Hayley said loudly. "Is she going to be all right?"

Her panicked tone brought the others to her side. They formed a protective flank around her.

"It wasn't fatal, but it isn't good," Pat said. "We're just trying to piece together what happened that night."

She went on to say that Hana had been found lying in the mud next to her car, her door flung open and her window smashed. As the officer explained, Hayley realized to her horror that Hana had had her accident the night she missed rehearsal.

But maybe it was no accident at all. Hayley bit her lip and said nothing.

"It was raining cats and dogs that night," Andy said. "Remember?"

"The roads were terrible," Sean agreed. "And if Hana was late, like she usually was . . ."

"Late?" Pat repeated. "She was late?"

"A bad habit," said Julianna. "She might have tried to make it to Hayley's in time, and crashed."

Pat wrote everything down. She looked at Hayley.

"I need to talk to you privately," she said.

"Hayley, are you okay?" Aidan wanted to know.

"I'm fine," Hayley said. "Kate, maybe you'd better talk to the manager."

Kate nodded and left. The others walked away, but lingered close by, probably hoping to catch snatches of the conversation.

"Wayne Boyer was also a member of your company," Pat said. "Do you know if he and Hana had any mutual enemies?"

Hayley shook her head. Of course they had no common enemy. They hardly knew each other! No common enemy, but a connection to Hayley herself that was deadly enough . . .

She didn't say this out loud.

"I don't understand," she said. "With the rain and all, wasn't it just a bad accident?"

"We have to cover all possibilities," Pat said.

Hayley pretended to think.

"As far as I know," Hayley said, "they didn't meet before I started Jackal. But I don't understand. If Hana is okay, why don't you ask her?"

"She's in a coma," Pat said simply. "Her family wants no contact from outsiders."

That explained the unanswered telephone.

"Poor Hana," Hayley said. "I hope you find out what happened to her. She was—*is* such a sweet kid!"

"So her brother told me," Pat said. She closed her notepad. "I'll be in touch."

When she was gone, Hayley bit her lip to keep from crying. Still, tears filled her eyes.

"It's okay, dear," Andy said. "I'm sure Hana's going to be fine!"

"But she thinks I've got something to do with it!" Hayley said.

"Oh, that's just a cop being a cop," Sean insisted. "Don't you worry. I'm sure Hana will have a perfectly logical explanation when she recovers."

Hayley looked around with big, frightened eyes. "But what if she doesn't?"

Aidan put his arms around her. "Don't think about that now, Hayley. She's going to be okay."

"You don't know that," Hayley insisted.

"I'm thinking positive," Aidan replied.

Kate came back. "I've squared things with the manager," she said. "We're all done for tonight."

Hayley took a deep breath. She knew she couldn't help Hana by getting hysterical.

"Then let's go home and rest up for tomorrow's performance," Hayley said. "Great job, guys. We'll dedicate tomorrow's show to Hana, okay?"

Everyone was in agreement, although Sean mumbled something about it seeming like Hana was dead already. They left one by one, Kate the last of the group.

"What did the manager say?" Hayley asked. "Is he upset?"

"He thinks it was just a routine investigation into an accident," Kate reassured her. "And that's probably just what it was. Until we find out, Hayley, don't make yourself crazy with guilt and worry!"

"I wish I could," Hayley said softly.

Kate gave her a hug. Aidan and Hayley left the restaurant with their arms around each other. Somehow, Hayley felt safer when she was with Aidan. If her tormentor were to show up suddenly, she'd have someone to help her defend herself.

As if you could defend yourself against a ghost . . .

As if Hana could defend herself . . .

Hayley brushed the thoughts aside.

"Why are you looking around?" Aidan asked. "Do you think he's hiding out here?"

"I don't know," Hayley said, gazing across the parking lot at the dark alley behind the restaurant.

Somehow, though, she knew Bruce wasn't here. She didn't feel . . .

She shivered. Aidan pulled her closer.

"Shouldn't feel cold," Hayley said. "It must be eighty degrees out tonight."

"My grandmother used to say that when you shiver, someone just walked on your grave."

Hayley winced. "That's terrible. It hits a little too close to home these days."

They got into Aidan's car. Although Hayley usually shared rides with Kate, her friend had deferred when Aidan offered to take Hayley to and from the restaurant. Hayley and Aidan had planned to stay at Hayley's house. He'd brought the dog there, too, at Hayley's insistence. There was no way she was going to give anyone a real chance at Lady.

Aidan turned on an oldies station, but kept it down so low they could barely hear it.

"Do you think I should get a lawyer?" Hayley asked out of the blue.

"Why?" Aidan inquired. "Because of a few questions from a cop? Hayley, she's probably questioning everyone Hana has had contact with in the past few weeks."

"But she also mentioned Wayne," Hayley said desperately. "She's trying to find a connection, and so far as I know, the only connection is me!"

"You've got friends, Hayley," Aidan said. "A lot of people would stick up for your character, and not just the company. You've spent a lot of time in Montauk over the years. No one who knows you would believe for a moment that you're capable of hurting anyone!"

"God, I hope you're right," Hayley said. She rubbed her eyes. "I'm so tired . . ."

"So take a rest," Aidan suggested. "I'll wake you up when we get home."

Hayley closed her eyes, but she didn't rest. She was too much on edge, too worried about Hana.

In the Intensive Care Unit of a small hospital, Hana Musashi lay very pale and still. The green lights of a monitor were the only proof that she was alive. Her aunt Mariko watched the screen, seeing a heart beating steadily, a pair of cartoon lungs blinking. She knew the low number beside the lungs indicated Hana was sleeping. Mariko was grateful for this. As long as she was sleeping, she wasn't in pain. Mariko prayed she'd stay that way for the night. She didn't think she could take much more of the fearful moaning sound Hana made when she started to come around.

Leo was off somewhere making arrangements to bring his niece back to the mansion. There was plenty of room in the north wing to set up a hospital room, where Hana could be watched over by a good Japanese nurse. Mariko knew that Leo wanted as much privacy as possible. Given his position as the head of a huge computer company, it wouldn't take long for word of this to reach the papers, and although he practiced all the social graces needed by an astute businessman, Leo craved solitude.

Hana stirred a little in her sleep. Mariko put aside the magazine she was skimming and leaned forward to look more closely at her niece. Her bruised, purple eyes made it hard to see how pretty she was. Prettier than many of the actresses Mariko had seen.

Maybe they'd been wrong to discourage her. If they'd been supportive, if one of them had gone along with her . . .

Mariko settled back again. There was no point in speculation.

"Sleep good, Hana-San," she whispered, closing her own eyes.

She drifted off to sleep, unaware that her niece was reliving the nightmare of her accident just then, only in a much more horrifying way.

Hana was under her car, watching rain that had somehow turned to blood, red droplets pouring from a bright golden sky.

This wasn't Long Island.

"This is hell," Hana whispered.

She watched a pair of boots circle the car. The boots became a pair of clawed feet. Huge talons flexed, a reptilian wing dragged along the blood-soaked mud.

Wayne Boyer was a dragon.

Not Wayne. Not a dragon. The devil had come to kill her.

There was a horrible screeching sound, and suddenly the car flew up and away from her, as if picked up by a tornado. Hana turned on her back and screamed as a huge, winged dragon swooped toward her, bloodied rain soaking its scales. It picked her up and carried her off, dropping her over a dark ocean. She fell and fell and fell . . .

Registered nurse Richard Knight, assigned to Hana Musashi for the night, looked up at the sound of a ringing bell. He hurried to her room to check her. Her heart rate was too high, but even as he entered her room it began to slow again. He knew she'd been dreaming, perhaps of the accident itself.

"Poor kid," he whispered.

He took care of her. Beside the bed, her aunt snored softly. Richard did not leave Hana's side until he was certain she was okay.

14

Hayley woke up with her back pressed against Aidan, bathed in the warm sunlight that streamed between the vertical blinds. Aidan's arms were so strong, and his body so warm, that she lay there for a long time with a contented smile on her face, dreamy. The kiss they had shared last night had only been the beginning. And it truly was a beginning—not just of a night of love, but of a new relationship. She felt very right and good about this. There was no feeling that she was betraying Jack's memory. If she had to justify herself at all, it would be to say that Jack of all people would want her to be happy. If only she could lay here with Aidan forever . . .

But Lady began to bark, a motorboat raced along the surface of the ocean, and somewhere a lawnmower started up noisily. It was time to get up.

She turned on her side, and propped her head on her

hand as she watched Aidan scrunch up his eyes and stretch away the last vestiges of sleep. She was smiling when he looked at her.

"What's so funny?" he asked.

"Nothing," Hayley said. "I'm just happy. I know I shouldn't be, with what happened to Hana and all, but I am. You're the best thing to happen to me in a long time. Maybe the only good thing."

Aidan didn't say a word, but pulled her close and kissed her. For a little while, they shared their love, not hearing a thing other than their own breathing. When they were done, Hayley cuddled close and said softly:

"Lady wants you."

"Uh-hmm."

"Maybe she needs to go out."

Aidan sighed.

"Probably," he said, rolling out of bed. He looked back at Hayley. "I'm beginning to appreciate my sister."

"Why?" Hayley asked, watching him reach for his jeans.

"She said there's never any time for grown-ups when a new baby comes," Aidan replied, pulling on his pants. "I think I get it now. Lady's like my new baby."

"I guess she is," Hayley agreed.

She got up herself and started to dress. Aidan went to take care of the puppy. When Hayley came into the kitchen, she found Aidan cleaning the cage.

"Too late," she said.

"Poor dog," Hayley said. "I feel cruel."

But Lady jumped around Hayley and wagged her tail, full of affection.

"Oh, she's okay," Aidan said. "We'll just take her for a longer walk to make up for ignoring her."

Hayley leaned down to pet the dog, accepting wet puppy-lick kisses with laughter.

"Can I take you out to breakfast?" Aidan asked.

Hayley straightened up.

"No, but I can take *you* out," she said. "There's a bagel place in town. We can walk along the beach until we get there. And when we're done, maybe we can try to see Hana?"

"Sure," Aidan said.

Hayley hooked a pair of sandals on her hand and opened the sliding door. Out on the deck, Aidan took off his sneakers, watching as Hayley carefully locked the door.

The sand was already warm on their bare feet, and they moved toward the cooler edge of the water. A distance ahead, Lady played with the tide and chased gulls. Hayley sighed, taking in the serenity of the Montauk coastline. She loved this place. Despite its tourist trade, it was still a quiet hamlet to her, a place that had brought her peace over the past few years. Having Aidan now only made things better.

Hayley tried to cling to this rare moment of contentment, to not think about the bad things that had been happening. But she couldn't do it. She was just too sensitive and caring to pretend, even for a little while, that everything was all right.

"I wonder how Hana is this morning," she said, sidestepping a forgotten pail and shovel.

"Maybe she's fine," Aidan said with optimism. "Maybe she's awake by now."

Hayley picked up a shell and studied it, as if the purple designs inside held a coded remedy to her worries.

"I hope so," she said. "God, I feel so guilty . . ."

"Don't talk like that," Aidan said. He reached out and took her hand, holding it tightly as they walked on. "You can't take responsibility for everyone."

Hayley shrugged. "I guess not. But I can't help thinking that Hana's accident has something to do with all the strange things that have been happening. What if the same person who killed Wayne and tried to poison you also attacked Hana? Jackal means a lot to me—too much to let someone stop me from running it. But that seems to be what he's trying to do, through the cast members. I just wish I could figure out why he's doing this to us!"

Aidan had no answer for her at that moment. They walked silently for a while, surrounded by the sounds of gulls and radios and laughing children. Hayley moved closer to Aidan. He put his arm around her shoulder.

"Things will be okay," she said. "There's something about this beach that makes me believe that."

"Good for you, Hayley."

"But I'm frustrated," Hayley went on. "If only I knew *when* things were going to be okay."

Aidan was thoughtful for a while. Finally, he said:

"Maybe you should consider closing Jackal for a while, at least, until the person who is doing all this is caught."

"Aidan, that could take a long time," Hayley said. "Is it really fair to cancel the bookings we have, when people are relying on us? What kind of reputation will that give us? More than that, wouldn't it be like saying he won? Because if someone is out to drive me out of business, putting the company on hold would be a victory for him."

Aidan put his arm around her.

"You're right, of course," he deferred.

Starting up Jackal Mystery Productions had only served to remind her how much she missed the theater. She could never let anyone take her life's work from her!

They'd reached a little path that cut between a pair of hotels and led into downtown Montauk. Aidan called Lady and put on her leash, holding her at his side as they walked to the bagel store. Hayley chose an egg bagel with ham and cheese, while Aidan asked for cinnamon raisin. The clerk gave him a piece of bacon for Lady.

They found a bench to sit on, set breakfast between them. Hayley sipped her hot chocolate and watched people walking by.

"I'm going to visit Hana this morning," she said. "It's Saturday, so I don't have work."

"Speaking of work," Aidan said, "I've got a program to work on at home. My proposals were approved."

"Even on Saturday?"

"The sooner I get it done, the sooner I get paid."

He put his arms around Hayley.

"Still, I wish I could stay," he said. "I hate to leave you alone."

"It's broad daylight," Hayley said. "Don't worry, Aidan."

He looked out the window at his dog, who had plunked down to sleep on the sidewalk.

"I could leave Lady with you," he suggested. "She isn't much, but she barks loud enough. She could warn you if someone was coming."

"Leave her," Hayley said. "The poor baby is tired. And we have fun together."

When they finished breakfast, they walked back to Hayley's house. Aidan carried Lady part of the way. After a little polite conversation, they kissed again, and finally said good-bye. For a few moments, Hayley felt nervous about being alone. Even the bright midday sun didn't help. But she fought the feeling and busied herself by getting ready to visit Hana. She washed away the sand from the beach, changed into shorts and a sleeveless top, then put Lady into her kennel.

"Be back soon," she promised.

She hated to leave the dog alone, but reasoned it

would be more dangerous to transport her around in a car in ninety-five degree weather.

It was a long, pleasant ride to Hana's hometown, one of the richer hamlets of the East End. Hana had never come across as someone with money. She wore little in the way of jewelry, and her clothes were nice, but nothing special. Hayley guessed she must live in one of the smaller houses in the area.

She had to double-check the address when she pulled up to a huge wrought-iron gate. Behind it, a brick house with numerous windows loomed against a backdrop of blue sky and the Long Island Sound. Hana lived *here*?

She got out of the car and went to the gate. A Siamese cat meowed at her from its perch atop the post, then jumped out of sight. The gate was unlocked, and there was no bell. Hayley pushed open the gate and walked onto a gravel path. The house seemed to be a mile away. Two horses grazed in the distance. In a garden, Hayley saw a peacock strutting proudly, its tail wide and beautiful. A smaller brown female pretended to be oblivious.

She reached a group of topiary trees. Movement behind a swan made her turn to see an elderly gentleman peering at her. His pruning sheers seemed frozen in mid-slice. Hayley smiled politely at him.

"Good morning," she said.

He didn't reply, but she could feel him peering at her as she moved on toward the house. At last, she reached the door, rang the bell, and waited.

A plump Japanese woman, dressed in a pink domestic uniform, opened the door and stared at her without greeting.

"Hi," Hayley said. "I'm Hayley Seagel. I'm a friend of Hana's."

"She's sick," the woman said. "She sees no one today."

"It's okay," said a young man's voice. "I'll take care of it."

The maid stepped aside, and Hayley greeted Hana's brother. At last, perhaps she would get some answers. Yoshi led her into a sitting room that was beautifully furnished with silk brocade and black lacquer. There were no cheap plastic imitations in this room. Hayley spotted a pair of swords mounted over the huge mantel, and guessed at once they were very old, and priceless.

"I heard that Hana was in an accident?" she said as a question. "How is she?"

Yoshi shook his head. "We're so worried about her. Someone saw a car stuck on the side of the road a few nights ago, when we had that terrible rainstorm. Thank God Hana had put her flashers on. The passerby called the police."

Hayley closed her eyes. Hana had been on the way to rehearsal. It was her fault Hana was hurt.

"When she went off the road," Yoshi continued, "her door popped open. The car has an automatic seatbelt, and when she fell out she got caught in it. It nearly strangled her."

"But the cop said she was dirty with mud," Hayley pointed out, "as if she'd been out of the car."

"That's something we can't explain," Yoshi said. "But there's a theory that mud flew into the car when her window broke. There's no indication that anyone . . . touched her."

Hayley closed her eyes. Could there possibly be a simple explanation? No, there was more to it. She felt it in her gut. Someone got after Hana . . .

"Is she going to be all right?

"We don't know," Yoshi said. "There was a loss of oxygen, and she's in a coma. We may never know what really happened to her."

"I'm so sorry."

"Not your fault," Yoshi reassured her. "It was an unfortunate accident."

It is my fault! I kept Jackal going, even though Wayne was murdered! Wayne, and maybe now Hana! It's my fault!

"Hayley?"

Hayley's heart pounded so hard that her eardrums were vibrating. She knew that this was no accident. No seatbelt had strangled Hana. Bruce was after her, the way he'd gone after Wayne.

"What's wrong?" Yoshi asked.

Hayley waved a hand at him. With a mumbled apology, she hurried from the house. She felt light-headed and confused, as if Bruce's evil influence had reached even this beautiful place.

She started to run, wanting to be as far away from Hana's home as possible.

15

All her life, Hayley had kept her encounters with the other world a deep secret. Even as a child, she had perceived that most people wouldn't really believe her. Ghosts were make-believe, elements of camp stories and Halloween fun. Nobody ever really saw a ghost.

She knew that her parents had watched her for a long time after she told them the number of the truck that hit Ricky. They pretended not to, but she was sensitive enough to know what it meant when they quickly averted their eyes as she walked into a room. Hayley knew they wouldn't understand about Ricky's appearance. It would upset her mother; her father would say it was all her imagination.

Nobody could ever explain how she suddenly knew the vehicle's number.

Years later, after the murders in Boston, no one understood how Hayley's personality had changed from deep depression and paranoia one day to acceptance and controlled anger the next. She never told a soul how Jack had appeared to reassure her that he and Kelly were okay. If she'd worried about ridicule as a child, she was doubly cautious as an adult.

But now, after what had happened to Hana, she knew she had to talk to someone. Maybe Kate and Aidan wouldn't understand. Maybe they'd try to come up with some lame explanation for what had happened. No matter, it would feel better to get her doubts into the open. So she called them both and asked them to meet her for dinner. She chose a restaurant near the Spice Rack, where they were performing tonight, so that they could go there directly after dinner.

"I'm surprised you didn't pick the Spice Rack," Aidan said as they sat down together.

"Too noisy," Hayley said. "I need your full attention. It's going to be very hard for me to talk. Besides, I didn't want the manager there to see how upset I am."

"Upset?" Kate asked. "What happened, Hayley?"

Hayley picked up her glass. Noticing the small but quick movements of the surface of the water, Hayley realized her hand was shaking and put the glass down again. God, how could she say this?

I think I'm being haunted.

"Take it slow, Hayley," Aidan said.

She looked at him and chewed her lip for a moment. He looked very concerned. So did Kate. It didn't seem they'd make fun of her.

"Do you remember the Shadow Man, Kate?" she asked bluntly. "The man under your bed?"

"Are you kidding?" Kate said. "I could never forget it. It seemed so real."

"I think it was real," Hayley said. "I think the giant rat on my patio was real, too."

She took a drink of water. Her bracelet clanged against the glass. Aidan took her hand in his to steady it.

"I think they were connected with Wayne's death and Hana's accident," she said.

"How can that be?" Kate asked. "The Shadow Man and the rat were dreams!"

"There was a rat taped to my window in the morning," Hayley reminded her. "Whoever did that also killed Wayne and tried to kill Hana."

Aidan leaned forward. "But Wayne was bitten by a snake, and Hana was in a car accident."

"I don't think either of those things happened the way we were told," Hayley said. "I think there's an evil force behind all this."

The waitress came back with their dinners, but no one seemed interested in food.

"Evil force?" Kate echoed. "You had thought Wayne was responsible, but now he's dead. Who, then?"

After so much misgiving and worry, Hayley answered the question now without hesitation.

"Bruce Donner."

"Who?" Kate seemed to have not heard.

Aidan reached for the ketchup and soaked his fries.

"I thought he was dead," he said.

"Yes, he's dead," Hayley said. She took a deep breath. "There's something I never told anyone, not even you, Kate. When Bruce hanged himself, he cut words into his chest, a message: WAIT FOR ME. Nobody knew about that, except a few people involved in the case. They kept it out of the papers. So tell me, how is it that somebody here on Lond Island, hundreds of miles away, knew to keep asking "Why didn't you wait for me?""

"Someone involved with the Boston case," Aidan suggested. "Some sicko who moved to Long Island and saw your name in the paper when you advertised for Jackal. He wanted to play sick games."

"Why?" Hayley asked. "I had no enemies in Boston."

"Someone close to Bruce?" Kate suggested. "Did he know anyone on the police force?"

Hayley's short laugh was full of dark humor.

"He was arrested a few times for being drunk," she said. "I'm sure they knew him. But he never mentioned any cop friends to me."

"Were you close?" Aidan asked.

"He was my mentor," Hayley said. "For all his problems, he helped me achieve success. I looked up to him like a big brother. I suppose I was so caught up in friendship that I never saw love."

She watched her friends, wondering what they thought of her. Kate looked confused as she pushed glazed carrots around her plate. Aidan ate well enough, but he was staring off at the window in thought. Hayley gave them time to think about what she'd said.

"I don't believe in ghosts," Kate said, finally, "but I do think something's going on. Is it possible we've been drugged? Aidan, did you ever get the results of your tests? Maybe the drug made you sick that night, too sick to even hallucinate?"

Aidan swallowed something quickly.

"I forgot about that," he said. "It was strange. The lab results came back negative. It seems I hadn't been poisoned that night after all."

"Oh, right," Hayley said sarcastically. "You just keeled over like that for no reason whatsoever."

"They said it was some helluva strong virus," Aidan said.

Kate held up her hand and looked at the scab on her finger.

"I wouldn't put much store in what labs have to say," she told them. "They found human saliva where a gull bit me."

Hayley felt chilled. Human saliva . . .

She'd been sitting with Kate when the gull attacked!

Bruce was getting at them through other sources. Through a gull, a rat, a snake . . .

Maybe through another human being? Had someone driven Hana off the road on purpose, someone as real as any of them?

"I want you to be careful," Hayley warned. "You're both my closest friends right now. Aidan's sickness might have been a warning. He might come after you again."

"What about Hana and Wayne?" Kate asked. "You only met them a few weeks ago."

"Also warnings, and threats," Hayley said. "I think he's going to come after all of the company before he gets to me."

Kate shivered violently. She put her arms around herself.

"I hope that Shadow Man doesn't come back again," she said. "God, I'm terrified of the bogeyman."

Aidan was eyeing her with disbelief. She tilted her head.

"Well, I am," she said. "Maybe not the bogeyman, but the idea of someone getting into my apartment at night. It's my phobia."

"Phobia," Aidan repeated. He looked at Hayley. "What are you most afraid of?"

"Getting sick, being poor," Hayley said. "I'm not afraid of dying. I know there's something after this. But . . ."

Aidan shook his head. "No, not that. I mean, do you have a phobia? Kate's afraid of something she calls the Shadow Man."

"Rodents," Hayley said slowly, beginning to understand his point. "I'm terrified of rodents."

Kate picked up on the idea at once. "Somehow, he's playing on our fears," she said.

"Right," Aidan agreed. "And I'll bet Wayne Boyer was afraid of snakes."

It seemed an exciting idea. But then Hayley said, "There's no connection to Hana's accident."

Aidan sat back and flagged the waitress. He asked for the check.

"We don't have time to discuss that," he said. "It's getting late."

"I'm for keeping this to ourselves while we investigate," Kate suggested.

Hayley nodded in agreement. "No use in upsetting everyone else."

"But shouldn't they be warned?" Aidan asked. "Is it ethical to keep it from them if they're in danger?"

"We'll figure out something to say," Hayley said, "without bringing up the supernatural. Nobody would believe it, anyway. You two barely believe me."

"You know I've always been a skeptic," Kate pointed out.

They split the check when it arrived and headed for the Spice Rack. On the way they discussed strategy, and finally decided how to present the problem to the others.

"We think someone might be trying to cause trouble," Hayley told the rest of the company. "It's possible he tried to poison Aidan and even drove Hana off the road to keep her from making it to the play."

She wouldn't mention Wayne Boyer's death.

Sean's eyes were wide. "I can hardly believe it."

"I can," Andy said. "There's a lot of competition out there."

"Whatever you think," Hayley said, "please be careful.

He seems to be very clever, and very quick. If he plans to strike, he'll do it with little warning."

A gasp made her turn to Julianna, who was holding Taylor in her arms.

"It would be better if you left Taylor at home from now on," Hayley said, "for her own safety. She really doesn't belong backstage anyway, Julianna."

"She belongs with me!" Julianna insisted.

Jamie, who had come with his wife and baby that night, stood behind Julianna and began to massage her shoulders.

"You know she's safe with me, honey," he said. He looked directly at Hayley. "Maybe it would be better if Julianna wasn't part of this group at all. I don't like the idea of someone coming after her. She's had enough problems in her life."

It was the first hint of something behind Julianna's obsession with the baby. Hayley made a mental note to talk Jamie later.

"Please don't quit," she said. "Julianna's so talented, a vital part of this company."

"I'm not quitting," Julianna said with determination, turning to look at her husband. "And I'm not leaving Taylor behind."

The baby began to cry. Julianna fished a bottle out of the diaper bag and went to a quiet corner of the room to feed the baby. Hayley leaned closer to Jamie to talk quietly.

"Is she all right?" Hayley asked. "She seems more worried about the baby than . . ."

"Than a normal mother?" Jamie whispered back.

"I didn't mean . . ."

Jamie waved a hand. "It's okay. Other people have noticed it too. It makes my mother crazy—Julianna won't let her babysit her own grandchild."

He sighed deeply. "We lost our first baby to SIDS. Julianna's never gotten over it."

"Oh, dear," Hayley said. "I had no idea . . ."

Jamie braved a half smile. "It's okay. You just keep Julianna coming here. It's the first time she's really gotten out, and it's good for her."

"She's good for Jackal," Hayley said.

Andy spoke loudly. "What are you two whispering about?"

"Just trying to think this out," Hayley lied. "It's a real mystery of our own, isn't it? I wonder which of us will be the first to solve it."

"I'll keep my eyes and ears open," Andy said.

"Me, too," Sean agreed.

"Just be careful," warned Aidan.

A glance at the clock told them it was time to get ready to perform. While the first part of the play was being staged, Kate took Hayley aside.

"I think it's time we expanded our cast."

"Now?" Hayley replied. "When our original group is being threatened? Do you think that's wise?"

"I have a feeling Julianna is going to back out eventually," Kate said. "With Hana gone, and then Julianna, there's only the two of us to play any female roles. And I think it would make more sense to have a larger group so that we can rotate. We didn't think of this when we started Jackal Mystery Productions because we had no idea it was going to be such a success. But you can see how the audience likes it. I have a feeling they're going to expect more from us."

Kate's logic made sense, but Hayley hated to put anyone else in danger.

"Let's do it by word-of-mouth," she said. "I'm afraid an ad in the paper would alert—whoever it is. We'll keep a backup roster. But I really don't want anyone new performing until they catch this guy."

"This guy," Kate repeated. "Does this mean you've given up on the idea of Bruce Donner?"

"No," Hayley said firmly. "I believe he's out there. He might be working through someone else."

A look of worry suddenly came over Kate's face.

"Could it be someone right here in our group?"

Hayley had no time to respond. Andy came off stage and Kate had to go on. She gave Hayley a look to say they'd talk about this later. Then she straightened her shoulders and marched out of the room. Her booming voice, with its thick German accent, sent the audience into giggles.

"Vas is dis?" she bellowed. "Villiam, you must put down der cards!"

"But I *must* place a bet!" Sean said dramatically. "If I don't, I'll die!"

"Of course you vill not die," Kate said.

Sean looked confused. "I won't?"

A patient smile from Kate the doctor.

"No."

Now Sean produced a huge knife.

"Then I shall kill myself! I can no longer live like this!"

"Nonsense!" said Kate, grabbing the knife. "It's only der prop in der play. You can't kill yourself mit a rubber knife! See?"

At this point, Kate was to repeatedly stab herself with the trick knife and show Sean that she was uninjured. Later, Kate's body would be found with multiple knife wounds, and Sean would be a suspect. Of course, several others in the play had motives, too. It would be up to the audience to guess "whodunit" at the end.

Hayley watched from the other room as Kate raised the knife, ready to strike herself.

Suddenly, everything seemed to grow dim. Hayley thought there was something wrong with the lights, until she realized that no one else was reacting. The air grew thicker and hotter. Hayley shivered; the sense that something was wrong overwhelmed her.

Without thinking, Hayley took a big step forward and tried to call out to Kate. It was too late.

The knife jammed into Kate's stomach. Blood oozed from the wound and Kate's eyes went wide. Somehow she managed to choke out:

"Guess it wasn't a fake."

She collapsed to the ground to a round of applause. The audience thought this was all part of the play.

"She's been stabbed!" Aidan cried, coming around the table. "Someone switched the knives."

Sean looked around in a panic, then ran off stage. Aidan picked up Kate and carried her off stage. This was not part of the play at all, but no one in the restaurant was aware of this.

"Oh my God," Hayley said. "She's really hurt herself!"

Kate stared up at everyone, her eyes wide with terror. "What . . . what happened?" she asked.

"Don't talk, dear," Andy said. "Jamie's gone to tell the manager he should call an ambulance."

"I don't . . ." Kate paused for a breath. ". . . want a . . . fuss. Then he'll . . . win this one."

"How did he switch the knives?" Sean asked. He felt terrible—he'd handed the weapon to Kate.

"I don't know," Hayley admitted. "But we've got to go on. Andy, it's your scene."

Andy nodded solemnly and went on. He wasn't supposed to act as if Kate had died; that scene didn't take place until later. But like a real pro, he improvised, pushing the play ahead a few scenes.

"I'm glad the old Kraut is dead!" he cried. "Thinks she's better than me with her fancy degrees!"

Inside the back room, Hayley was holding Kate's hand. Aidan took the other and they both encouraged Kate to keep her eyes open. The paramedics showed up quickly, entering through a back door so as not to disturb the audience. Hayley decided to take Kate's car and follow the ambulance.

"Handle things here," she told Aidan. "My character was never set up as a suspect, anyway. The play will work fine with just the rest of you."

At the hospital, she paced the waiting room, unable to settle herself. Her thoughts were a jumble of anger and worry. Finally, she stood still and concentrated on a watercolor print hanging on the wall. She had to focus her thoughts!

"Think, Haley," she whispered. "Think about this!"

You know who he is. He was supposed to be there that day.

Hayley realized Jack's words had something to do with her old crew. If she could only find the connection between the people she'd worked with years ago and the people in her present company, she'd understand. She'd . . .

Someone was tapping her shoulder.

Hayley turned to see an intern gazing at her through thick glasses.

"You're Miss Reising's sister?"

"Sister?"

Hayley realized Kate might have pretended she was a family member so Hayley could get information. She played along.

"Sister-in-law," she said. "Is she okay?"

"Just fine," the intern told her with a weary smile. "The knife had a short blade, and it missed all vital organs. She'll hurt for a while, and we'll want to keep her for observation, but she'll be fine."

"Can I see her?"

The intern showed the way, leading her to a small curtained-off area.

Kate looked very pale, but she managed a smile when she saw Hayley.

"Guess I play a better murder victim than we thought," she said.

Hayley laughed, but only briefly.

"God, Kate," she said. "I don't know what I would have done if he'd really killed you."

"Hayley, I don't believe I was attacked by a ghost," Kate said. "Someone hates Jackal, someone real."

She grimaced.

"Are you okay?" Hayley asked worriedly.

"I guess," Kate said. "Just a little sore when I move the wrong way. Hayley, listen, I don't understand what's been happening to us. But please, be careful. He's come close to killing me, and Aidan, and maybe Hana. Whoever 'he' is, he might even have set that snake on Wayne Boyer."

She looked at her monitor, watching the green images for a few moments before speaking again.

"Maybe you should shut down . . ."

"No!"

"Just for a while," Kate said. "We're all in too much danger."

"I don't think it's going to make any difference," Hayley said. "I might have to delay some performances because I don't think Julianna and I can handle all the roles. But delaying doesn't mean quitting. Bruce might have taken this battle, but damn it, the war's going to be mine!"

"Hayley, Bruce is . . ."

Kate began to cough violently. The monitor went crazy, the previously steady green blip on the screen jumping in wild spikes. A nurse came in and shooed Hayley away. Hayley watched from down the hall as a doctor rushed in.

A short time later, they wheeled Kate to another room. Kate had an oxygen mask on now, and her eyes were closed.

Hayley cornered an intern.

"I thought you said she was okay?"

"It's the strain," he insisted, then hurried after the group surrounding Kate's gurney.

Dejected, feeling she was of no help, Hayley turned and left the room. As she was walking down the hall, she heard someone calling her. She turned to see Pat Alan.

"I need to ask you some more questions," the police officer said. She indicated a waiting area. "Let's sit down. Your company seems to have a jinx on it," Pat said. "Wayne Boyer, Hana Musashi, now Kate Reising."

"The restaurant called you?"

"An officer always responds to an emergency call," Pat said. "The manager contacted us. A knife attack is a serious offense, Ms. Seagel."

"She . . . wasn't attacked," Hayley said, uncertain how to handle this. "The knife was switched, somehow," she continued. "I don't know how anyone could have gotten at it."

"Do you keep the props?"

Hayley shook her head quickly. "No, they're at Julianna Wilder's house. We often practice there. Do you have the knife?"

"That's the strange part," Pat said. "The manager picked up the knife, and it was a trick knife, after all."

"But she was bleeding so much," Hayley said. "They just took her upstairs."

Pat looked at the large window, darkened into a mirror by the night. She adjusted her cap.

"A man is covered with snakebites," she said, not to Hayley, "but there's no venom in him. Still, he died of a heart attack. A woman is in a coma after a serious car accident. Another woman is nearly killed with a trick knife."

Now she looked directly at Hayley.

"Can you make a connection?" she asked. "Do you know what's going on here?"

Bruce Donner.

"No," Hayley lied. "I can't think who'd want to hurt these people. With the exception of Kate, whom I've known for years, I only met them all a few weeks ago! I hope you don't think I'm doing all this."

"No, I don't," Pat said. "But I do think you're holding back information. That could get you into a lot of trouble, Hayley."

"What do you mean?"

Pat checked her reflection again, as if her double might have answers for her questions.

"Since you're the head of a company where numerous people are being hurt," Pat said, "suspicion might fall on you. If I were you, I'd do whatever I could to find the real culprit, Hayley."

"I'm trying," Hayley said. She'd noticed she was on a first-name basis with the cop now. "I'm trying, Pat, but I just can't think of anyone."

"Try harder," Pat said, standing. "Because, next time, the questions may not be so tolerant."

She started for the door. "Be careful."

Hayley watched her go, her heart pounding. As Pat went out, Aidan came in, moving quickly, an uneasy look on his face. Hayley hurried over to him.

"She said I'm going to be in trouble," Hayley said. "Things are looking too suspicious."

Aidan put his arms around her and held her tightly for a few moments.

"Maybe you'd better fill me in," Aidan said.

Hayley told him everything.

"Sounds like she was just doing her job," he said. "But never mind that for now. How's Kate?"

"They had to take her upstairs," Hayley said. "I don't know what's going on. When the restaurant manager gave the knife to the police, it was a prop again. Bruce switched it twice! Oh, Aidan . . ."

She fought back tears. "What am I going to do?"

"Let's find a coffee shop and talk," Aidan said.

They walked into the parking lot together.

"Are you up to driving?"

"I'm okay," Hayley insisted. "I'll follow you."

A short time later, they were seated across from each other in a booth at a diner. Aidan ordered coffee and a bagel; Hayley just had hot chocolate.

"I had kind of a crazy idea when I was coming to the hospital," Aidan said as he buttered the bagel. "Then again, all things considered, maybe it's not so crazy."

Hayley leaned forward, her hands wrapped around the cocoa mug.

"Tell me," she said. "I need any help you can offer."

"A séance," Aidan said simply.

Hayley straightened up, backing away from the sting of being teased. She was about to reprimand Aidan for patronizing her when she realized that there was no glint of humor in his eyes. He was dead serious.

"A séance," she repeated.

Aidan nodded. "Look, I know it's the kind of thing you mess around with at parties and at camp when you're a kid. But if Bruce really is out there, this may be a way to corral him."

Hayley felt as if a great burden had been lifted from her.

"Then you believe me?"

"I believe something profane is going on here," Aidan said. "We need to bring it, or him, to our level. What do you think?"

"It could be very dangerous," Hayley said. "You've seen what he can do."

"I'm not afraid of him," Aidan insisted.

"I sure as hell am," Hayley admitted. "But I'm not going to run from him forever."

She reached across the table and took his hand.

"Let's do it," she said with determination.

16

No one in the cast of "Snake Eyes" knew that there was a killer among them. They only saw each other's familiar faces. But one face was a mask, hiding a dark spirit that was growing more and more vengeful. It was all he could do not to laugh when the knife had sunk into Kate's stomach. The naive fools had never suspected a switch.

The look of shock on Kate's face had delighted him, but not as much as he'd delight in her final destruction. But for now, there were others to drive out of his way.

Who next? The kid? The old guy?

Julianna, so tall and beautiful?

And her baby.

He smiled at the reflection he saw in his mirror. He knew exactly where he was going to strike next.

* * *

Jamie Wilder stood at the doorway of the nursery and watched Julianna rock Taylor to sleep. His wife looked so serene, in her long white robe with her freshly washed hair hanging long and wet over her shoulders. Jamie thought she was the most beautiful woman he'd ever seen; he loved her so much. It hurt him to see how obsessed she was with the baby. He admitted part of his pain was jealousy, but also knew that some of Julianna's fixation on Taylor came from the guilt that had been eating away at her for two years.

Their first child had been a little boy named Eddie. He'd seemed robust and healthy until, at the age of eleven months, Julianna found him lifeless in his crib one morning. The doctors had called it SIDS. A counselor tried to reassure them that it wasn't their fault, their families offered support, but Julianna wasn't convinced. As far as she was concerned, Eddie would still be alive if she'd gotten up to check him in the night.

Hayley Seagel didn't know that Julianna left her job at Radio City Music Hall because of a breakdown, not because she'd become pregnant with Taylor. To Julianna, Taylor was a godsend, a second chance. Nothing would happen to this baby. At first she kept the newborn with her at all times, even taking her into bed. But when Jamie expressed worry that she might get smothered, Julianna put her in a crib. She spent an hour each night putting the baby to sleep, and woke up countless times to check on her. It amazed Jamie that Julianna had the strength to run a household, let alone be part of a theater company.

"Coming to bed?" he asked gently.

"A few more minutes," Julianna whispered. "She's almost off."

Taylor wiggled and yawned.

"Oh, Jamie," Julianna said. "Look at her. Isn't she an angel?"

"You're both my angels," Jamie said.

He stood there for a while longer, until Julianna finally got up and set Taylor in her crib. He knew his wife would be back in here before she finally drifted off to sleep, but the thought of having only a short time in bed with his wife didn't stop him from cuddling up to her once they were under the covers. He kissed her face, her neck . . .

Julianna rolled on top of him, her body warm against his. As if Taylor was completely gone from her mind, they loved each other. There was no rush, and it was perfect, but when they were finished, Julianna got up and pulled on her robe. Jamie didn't ask where she was going. It was always the same. He would stay awake until she got back, then he'd ask about Taylor, and they'd both settle in for a few hours of sleep.

I feel really tired, he thought. *I don't think I can stay awake . . .*

Something pulled Jamie into an instant, deep sleep.

The nursery was just beyond the bathroom. Julianna left the door slightly ajar so she could hear Taylor in the night. Now she pushed the door open all the way, and froze.

Someone was standing over the baby's crib!

Julianna screamed as a stranger looked up at her, hands clamped around the crib-rail. His eyes were red in the dim glow of the night light. Julianna could see madness in them, and hatred.

"Get away from my baby!" Julianna screamed, lunging forward.

With one large hand, the stranger picked up the baby by the front of her sleeper. She dangled in the air, legs kicking, back bent, wailing.

Julianna grabbed for her daughter, but with an evil laugh the man jerked the baby from her at the last possible moment. Momentum slammed Julianna into the wall beside the baby's crib. A cross-stitched plaque proclaiming Taylor's birth crashed to the floor.

The stranger held the baby against his chest, facing outward. Taylor wiggled and screamed in outrage. Julianna stumbled for the door and yelled down the hall:

"Jamie! Jamie, help!"

She knew her husband would come at once. Strong, reliable Jamie. He'd take care of things. He always did.

He didn't come.

"Jamie!"

"Jamie is gone," the invader said. "There's nothing he can do for you. I've got your little brat now."

Frantically, Julianna scanned the room for anything she could use as a weapon. But she'd always surrounded the baby with soft, safe things. Not a sharp point or a hard object in sight.

She had only herself and her instincts to use to protect her young. Like a mother bear, she jumped at the man again, long fingernails at the ready. He threw the baby to the floor and grabbed her. With all-consuming terror, Julianna felt herself rising into the air. She watched as the ceiling came closer and closer to her face. Crazily, she realized she was bent backward now, just as Taylor had been. *She* was dangling like a baby.

"Let me go!"

Struggling, she twisted her head around ...

... and saw that there was nothing holding her up.

"Nnnnoooo!!!!"

She grabbed at an old light fixture and cried out in horror as her weight ripped it from the ceiling. A moment later, something slammed into her from below, and her face smashed into the ceiling. Pain shot through her and she tumbled to the floor.

She looked up through clouded vision to see Taylor

rising, as if by her own power, from the floor. Julianna screamed, reaching out to her.

"Not my baby! Oh God, *not my baby!*"

Suddenly, a ball of beautiful blue and white light appeared in the room. It swirled gently around the baby, completely enveloping her, carrying her down, into her crib. Julianna tried to pull herself to her feet, but she was frozen solid. She saw Taylor laid down gently on the crib mattress, unharmed. A moment later, the blue and white light vanished.

Julianna was able to move now, but as she struggled to her feet another light appeared, a hideously ugly beacon of black and red. It flew at her, striking her as hard as a hurricane wind, knocking her back against the wall. She fell to the floor, unconscious.

A baby was crying. Hayley knew she had to get to it, to save it from a horrible death. Bruce was going to kill it . . .

She found herself in the basement of Julianna's house. All the cast members of Jackal were there, even Wayne, Hana, and Kate. Wayne's skin was mottled in reaction to the snake's poison. There were black circles under his eyes. He smiled at Hayley.

"No one else can write for you," he said.

"Especially not me," Aidan put in.

"Aidan . . ."

Julianna floated toward her, as if her feet weren't touching the ground. She was dressed in a glittery dance costume.

"Has anyone seen Taylor? I can't find Taylor."

Upstairs, the baby was screaming.

"Julianna, she's upstairs, crying."

"Has anyone seen Taylor? I can't find Taylor."

"She's upstairs!"

Blood started gushing from Julianna's nose.

"Has anyone seen ..."

. *Someone tapped Hayley on the shoulder. She turned to find herself standing in her old Boston apartment, facing Jack and Kelly.*

"The baby is okay," Kelly promised. "But the danger gets closer."

"Bruce ..."

"He's strong," Jack said. "We can't ... always ... fight him ..."

"How do I get rid of him?"

"Destroy the other," Kate said. "The mortal one."

"Who?"

"You know who he is," Jack said. "He was supposed to be there that day."

"Damn you, *what* day?"

Aidan, awakened by Hayley's cry, rolled over and took Hayley into his arms.

"You're shaking," he mumbled sleepily. "Bad dream?"

"Horrible," Hayley said, cuddling against him. "Something was wrong with Taylor and I couldn't get Julianna to understand. Wayne was there, too, and you, and everyone else."

She took a deep breath to calm herself.

"Then Jack and Kelly came," she went on. "Kelly said the baby was okay. Jack said Bruce was too strong to fight, that I had to go after 'the mortal one' to destroy him."

"The mortal one?" Aidan echoed.

"I don't understand," Hayley said. "He keeps saying: 'You know who he is. He was supposed to be there that day.' But he never tells me what the hell he means."

Aidan held her tighter. "It must be important if he keeps repeating it. We've got to help him tell us. That's why we have to have the séance."

"As soon as Kate is better," Hayley said. She thought about the strange gull, and the knife switch that had nearly killed her. "I think Bruce has been in contact with her."

"We'll wait," Aidan said. "But I hope it doesn't take her too long to get out of the hospital. I don't think we have a lot of time."

Hayley sighed wearily. "I think you're right. We've got to fight Bruce as soon as we can."

She felt an overwhelming unease rising in her and pushed herself as close to the strength of Aidan's warm body as she could, to try to repel it.

"Dear Lord," she whispered. "I hope no one else is hurt because of me."

When Jamie woke to find Julianna's side of the bed empty, he got up quickly and went to investigate. He found Julianna lying on the floor of the nursery, unconscious. Cursing himself for falling asleep so easily, he gently turned her over and saw that both her eyes were blackened and blood had congealed around her nose, which was obviously broken.

"Julianna, wake up," he said firmly.

She didn't respond.

"Julianna?"

Now her long eyelashes fluttered. Then her blue eyes were staring up at him in terror. She grabbed at him.

"Ban hab Tawa!"

Jamie shook his head.

"Taylor's fine," he said.

"No!"

He helped her to her feet. They looked into the crib. Taylor was sound asleep. Without hesitation, Julianna grabbed her. It was going to be like Eddie. Taylor wasn't going to wake up. Taylor was going to be cold and still . . .

Taylor was crying.

Half smiling with relief, half weeping, Julianna turned to her husband.

"Subone attacked us."

"What?" Jamie asked in disbelief. "How? I didn't hear a thing."

Julianna, cradling Taylor against her, rocked back and forth and glared at her husband.

"Where were you?"

"In our room," Jamie said. "Asleep."

"I was scweabing and you slept?"

"Julianna, your nose . . ."

"The hell wib my nose! Why didn't you help me?"

Jamie didn't know what to say to her. If she'd been attacked, why hadn't he heard? Had it been real? She'd had terrible dreams after Eddie died. Night terrors, the therapist called them, where'd she go crashing through the house in search of their son. Once she'd fallen down the stairs.

He remembered from the counselor that the way to deal with this was to help her talk about it.

"Tell me what happened."

Speaking in a nasal voice, rocking Taylor all the while, Julianna told him about the attack, about the beautiful blue and white light and the ugly red and black one. At one point, Jamie found himself looking up at the ceiling. He wasn't surprised that the fixture was intact. But there was blood on the wall beside Taylor's crib.

"Look, honey," he said. "I think you might have imagined someone in here. Colored lights fighting over our daughter? That's surely a sign it was a dream!"

"It was no dream," Julianna insisted.

"You've been working so hard lately, between running

the house and acting. You were exhausted. I think you must have walked into the wall."

"He was here!"

"But the ceiling light isn't broken!"

Julianna clutched Taylor, who had fallen asleep again. Why didn't Jamie believe her?

Jamie couldn't stand to see her so distressed. Finally, he said, "I'll call the police. They can check things out for us."

"They aren't going to find anything," Julianna said. "It was some kind of spiritual encounter."

"Ghosts?" Jamie said. "Suddenly you believe in ghosts?"

Julianna turned away from him. Wanting to do the most practical thing, Jamie left the room to call the police.

Within an hour's time, the police had come and gone. They found no signs of forced entry, and tended to agree with Jamie that Julianna had broken her nose by accident. One suggested a trip to the emergency room. Packing up the baby, the family headed for the hospital. Over Julianna's protests, Jamie dropped Taylor at his mother-in-law's house, giving her a brief explanation of the night's events.

The emergency room was quiet at this hour and Julianna was cared for at once. By now, she'd calmed down quite a bit. Maybe Jamie was right. Maybe she had only dreamed the whole thing. No, that wasn't right. It had felt too *real*. No matter what Jamie, or the police, or even the doctors said, she knew it had happened. And there was no way in hell it was going to happen again. She'd kill anyone who even *looked* at Taylor in a strange way!

They were getting stronger. It infuriated him that they'd interfered tonight. Somehow, they'd combined what little power they had to pull him away from the baby. Why did they care so much about the little brat?

He knew that it was only a matter of time before they grew too powerful for him to fight. He had to work quickly, choose his next victim, and strike.

He stared at the reflection in the mirror, one that had grown so familiar that he hardly remembered what his real face used to look like. He smiled, but in his heart there was only festering blackness.

Bruce knew a way to get rid of Julianna, and maybe one or two of the others. It would be interesting to see how many he could take out in one shot.

17

Hayley was tempted to call Julianna and ask after Taylor. But what excuse could she make? She certainly couldn't tell Julianna about her dream, not considering Julianna's obsession with the baby.

"Probably make accusations," Hayley mumbled as she tied on a pair of running shoes.

Aidan moaned, turning over in the bed. He squinted at her.

"Whajja say?"

"I was thinking about Taylor," Hayley replied.

"Why?" Aidan asked. "Still thinking about that dream?"

Hayley wasn't really sure that it had been only a dream. But she didn't want to bother Aidan with her worries. At least, not until she was sure they were justified. She gave him a kiss. "Go back to sleep, lazybones. Some of us around here are keeping in shape."

"Some of us around here think sleeping late on a Sunday is a sacred thing," Aidan mumbled into his pillow.

The solitude of the beach in the early morning gave Hayley plenty of time to think. She went over the past few weeks, from her dream about the rat to Kate's 'accident.' Something had happened to almost everyone in her company.

She veered around a piece of driftwood. Some people would wonder why she hadn't gone to the police earlier, kept them involved. But how do you tell authorities who deal with evil in its most human form that the man stalking you has been dead for five years?

Hayley rarely attended church, but on the quiet beach that morning she prayed. She prayed for Kate, and for Hana, she prayed that Wayne was at peace. In the end, she prayed for herself, for the strength she would need to fight Bruce Donner's malevolent spirit.

As Hayley was jogging along the beach, Andy Constantino had settled into his favorite armchair to read the Sunday paper. He pulled off the plastic wrapper and let it fall open on his lap. The entire thing was wrapped in grocery circulars. Years ago, he would have passed these to his wife so she could clip coupons. But Sophia was gone now, and he himself had never seen the point of bothering with nickles and dimes. He dropped the sheets beside his chair, then separated the main part of the paper from everything else.

The headline, big and black, seemed to jump off the page.

"RADIO STATION DESTROYED IN FIRE."

Andy closed his eyes. Another station, like WDEM so long ago. He hoped no one had been hurt.

Opening his eyes, he began to read the article. By the

second line, he felt something congeal in the pit of his stomach. By the fifth, he was shaking so badly he had to put the newspaper down on the coffee table and lean forward to read it.

"At about 12:15 A.M., firefighters responded to an anonymous call, alerting them that radio station WDEM was ablaze."

WDEM! How could it be possible! Was there another WDEM here on Long Island?

"This is crazy," Andy said.

He forced himself to read more. It sickened him to learn that the bodies of a woman and a baby had been found in the rubble after the fire had been put out. The fire marshal couldn't explain why they were there at such a late hour, and an investigation was pending.

Andy rubbed his eyes wearily. It had the same name, but of course it wasn't the same station. WDEM had been closed for years, and it wasn't even in New York! And even if it had been a parallel crime, he knew that no one had died when he had . . . when his own station had burned down long ago.

He settled back with the paper again and turned the page. His own photograph, taken about twelve years earlier, took up a fourth page.

"HAVE YOU SEEN THIS MAN?"

"Andy Constantino, suspected arsonist in the burning of station WDEM, is being sought by . . ."

"No, it's a joke!"

Andy turned the page.

There was another picture of him, with the same questioning headline.

On the next page, another.

And another.

And another.

The entire paper was filled with repetitions of the same page, all demanding to know the whereabouts of Andy Constantino, arson suspect.

"It's a sick, sick joke!" Andy cried, tossing the paper aside.

He ran into his bathroom and threw up, sickened by the memory of that long-ago fire. Who knew about it? Who wanted to torment him in this way?

At the hospital, Kate was sitting up in bed reading her own newspaper. There wasn't a single story about any fire within its many pages. The front headline spoke of the president's trip to Asia. She was skimming the story when Hayley and Aidan walked into the room.

"Look at all this," Hayley said. A huge bunch of balloons hung suspended in one corner, and there were flowers on the windowsill.

"The balloons are from the people at the Captain's Chair," Kate said, referring to the antique store where she worked. "And the flowers are from Sean."

"Sean!" Hayley said in surprise. "I feel ashamed, Kate. I should have thought of it, too."

"Both of us should have," Aidan said.

Hayley pulled up a chair. Aidan leaned against the windowsill.

"It's just that we were hoping you'd be out of the hospital quickly," Hayley added. "What's the prognosis?"

Kate winced. "Don't use doctor words, Hayley. I've had enough of doctor words."

They all laughed.

"So, when are you getting out?" Aidan asked.

"Maybe tomorrow," Kate said. "They don't generally release people on Sunday. Probably interferes with someone's golf game. I'm stuck here another night."

"Well, maybe we forgot flowers," Hayley said, "but if you'd like, we can bring back dinner."

Kate's eyes widened hungrily.

"Oh, please do," she said. "Two slices of pizza with sausage and pepper and onions."

"You got it," Aidan promised.

As if a switch had been flipped, conversation stopped. There was only so much small talk they could make when so much was on their collective minds. Finally, Hayley spoke.

"I'm sorry this happened to you, Kate," she said.

"Don't be," Kate said. "You couldn't have known. I just don't understand how the knife could have been replaced."

Hayley straightened herself, looking across Kate's bed to Aidan. At once, Kate understood the exchange.

"Oh, you don't still think there's a ghost involved here, do you?"

"Aidan thinks we should have a séance," Hayley blurted out.

Kate rolled her eyes. "A séance? Two grown people?"

"Three, we hope," Aidan said. "Look, I know you think this is crazy. But you've got to admit there are a lot of things we can't explain here."

Kate leaned back on her pillow, closing her eyes.

"Maybe we should leave, Aidan," Hayley said.

"I'm not tired," Kate insisted. "I'm thinking."

A few moments later, she opened her eyes again.

"All right, I'll do it," she said. "But only because I think it will help you see that nothing at all supernatural is going on. You've got a stalker, Hayley. Instead of having a séance, you should be talking to the police."

Hayley wanted to argue with her, to tell her she couldn't make judgments when she wasn't the one having recurring nightmares or seeing her friends hurt one

by one. But she realized that Kate was trying to cooper-
ate with her, and held back her words. Instead she met
her halfway.

"If nothing comes of this," she said, "then I promise I
will call the police. It's possible they haven't made any
connections between Hana's accident and Wayne's death.
They certainly don't know about some of the other
events, like Aidan's being poisoned or that gull attacking
you . . ."

"Or the Shadow Man," Kate offered, her eyes growing
distant.

"Whether it's by our own hands," Hayley vowed, "or
with the help of the police, we will stop this man."

She took Kate's hand, Aidan took the other one, and
the three offered each other a moment of strength.

After leaving the hospital, Hayley and Aidan drove to
the Musashi place to ask about Hana. The servant who
answered the door said that Yoshi wasn't there, and that
Mr. and Mrs. Musashi were busy.

"We've come to ask about Hana," Hayley said.

The plump woman, the same servant who had greeted
Hayley the other day, peered hard at them.

"Please," Aidan said, "we're her friends."

"Hana is very sick," the servant told them. "Doctors
are here day and night. There is nothing more I can say."

With that, she shut the door.

"Cold fish," Aidan said.

As they walked away from the mansion, Hayley
looked up at the windows. Which one was Hana's? Was
she safe, in both her mind and her body? Bruce could get
to her even now . . .

She was so preoccupied she nearly tripped over a turtle
that was crossing the road. Aidan helped her steady herself, then picked up the animal and put it on the grass.

"She'll be okay," he said, insightful. "With all the money these people have, I'm sure they're keeping a close watch on her."

"I can't help my concern," Hayley said. "If Bruce had anything to do with this, then it's my fault."

"You're doing it again," Aidan said. "Blaming yourself."

"Okay, okay!" Hayley cried. "Not another word. Aidan, I need to clear my head anyway. Maybe if I give myself something else to think about, I'll come back with fresh ideas."

Aidan put his arm around her shoulder.

"Do you play tennis?" he asked. "I could go for a good match."

"I play a little," Hayley said, "but I'm not that good at it."

A short time later, they were enjoying a friendly game. Aidan saw that Hayley was hitting the ball harder and harder. He knew she was venting her anger through this game. They played until they were tired, and then went to Hayley's to swim in the ocean while Lady played on the beach. After sharing the refreshing warmth of a shower, they collapsed into bed together.

Hayley woke up and turned to put her arms around Aidan. But it was Jack who turned to her.

"Oh, Jack, I'm sorry! I thought you were . . ."

"He's growing stronger, Hayley," Jack warned. "There's no time."

"It's Bruce, isn't it?" Hayley asked. "Tell me if it's really Bruce who's doing this."

Jack stared at her for a moment, then nodded.

"And someone else," he said. "Someone on your side."

"Who?" Hayley asked. "Jack, stop playing games with me! I need to know who my enemies are!"

"You know him," Jack said. "You know who he is. He was ..."

"Don't say that again!" Hayley snapped. "Say his name! For God's sake, just say it out loud!"

But Jack wouldn't, or couldn't. Something was stopping him.

"You have to fight him, Hayley," Jack said. "You have to fight him now."

"I love you, Jack," Hayley said. "I'll always love you."

God, what if he hated her now because she was in bed with Aidan?

But she wasn't, was she? It was her beloved Jack who held her.

"Aidan is me," Jack said.

"Jack ..."

"Jack ..."

Hayley heard herself say the word out loud. She was awake, she knew, but she was afraid to turn and look next to her. Bruce might be there, as he'd been another night. He might have cut into her dream to stop Jack from talking to her. He might be ready to hurt her ...

With a deep sigh, Aidan rolled over in his sleep and put his arms around Hayley. Relief that Bruce had left her alone this time was so overwhelming that Hayley suddenly started to cry. At first, the tears were quiet. But then anger and frustration grew, and before she could stop herself she was sobbing enough to awaken Aidan.

He didn't ask why she was crying. Instead, he held her and spoke soothingly.

"I hate him so much," Hayley sobbed. "I hate him so much!"

18

On Monday, Hayley called up the restaurants they had booked and explained the situation. Everyone was disappointed but understanding. In a way, she was glad Jackal was a new company and had only a few bookings. It made things go more smoothly.

When she picked up the phone to dial the last number on her list, the receiver emitted a screeching noise that was so annoying she had to hang up. A moment later, she picked up the receiver again to hear a normal dial tone.

"Must have been a bad connection," she said.

She dialed the restaurant. Before anyone picked up on the other end, the line filled with indistinct voices, all speaking at once and impossible to understand. It was like listening to the voices of a thousand spirits.

"God, he's got me seeing ghosts everywhere," Hayley

said as she hung up the phone. "It's just a few crossed connections!"

With her hand still on the receiver, the phone rang. Hayley picked it up at once.

The voices were back again, mumbling, only their inflections bearing any resemblance to speech.

It was one thing to dial into a party line by accident: It was another to have a party line return a call.

Hayley listened for awhile, mesmerized. The voices had a strange, lulling effect. She heard a word . . .

"Wait."

Wait for me.

"Bruce?" It hardly seemed like her own voice, but she knew she had spoken.

There was no reply. The voices had stopped instantly, replaced by the horrid screeching that had made her hang up the phone before. She cringed and slammed down the receiver. She guessed Bruce didn't want her to make that last call, but why?

A cold chill washed over her, the feeling there was someone in the room with her. She swung around, expecting Bruce to be standing behind her. She was alone.

"Cut it out," she told herself. "It's broad daylight! There's nothing to be afraid of!"

Is that what Hana thought? Is that what Wayne thought?

"Stop watching me!" Hayley cried out. "Leave me alone!"

She grabbed her eyes and purse and ran out of the house. If she couldn't get through to the restaurant on the phone, she'd drive there. Anything to get out of the house!

As she drove along the quiet road in front of her house, she passed a man in a black jogging suit, pulling a wagon full of charred pieces of wood. But when she looked into her rearview mirror, he was gone. There were no turnoffs he could have used, only private property and woods.

"Damn you, Bruce," Hayley whispered.

Farther down the road, a small boy stood waving, his hand moving as slowly as if through water. He stared without smiling, his face pale.

Hayley didn't stop. She could only think of the naked man she'd hit a while back, the one who had disappeared. This time, when she looked into the mirror, the boy had turned into a deer that bounded across the road.

Three teenagers in bathing suits floated in front of her car. She slammed the brakes . . .

. . . and went right through them.

"Bruce, stop it!" she cried, knowing he was causing these visions.

She had reached the edge of downtown Montauk. Now the people she saw were real, living. The visions had stopped and did not occur again during the rest of the ride to Sayville. She found the restaurant without any trouble and went inside to take care of business.

To her surprise, the manager told her that someone had already explained the situation.

"I'm sorry you won't be able to work with us," she said. "But I do understand. What a terrible tragedy!"

"Tragedy?" Hayley didn't understand. "Mrs. West, who came to talk to you?"

"Let me see," Mrs. West said, sliding glasses up her long nose. She opened a notebook and began riffling through bits of paper. "Oh, it's here somewhere. He was here just about an hour ago."

The same time as the phone problems, Hayley thought.

"Oh, here it is," Mrs. West said. "Donner. The man's name was Bruce Donner."

Hayley felt the room spin. She grabbed hold of the woman's desk to steady herself.

"Did he ... what did he say?"

"Oh, he explained that one of your actresses had lost a baby. I can't imagine a more terrible tragedy! That poor woman. If anything had happened to one of my children when they were growing up ..."

Hayley barely heard her. The room was beginning to spin around, terror pulling her into a vortex. Baby?

"You be sure to give those poor parents my condolences," Mrs. West was saying.

Hayley mumbled a response. The only baby she knew of was Julianna's. Bruce had gotten to Taylor. Oh God, she should have called! She should have checked!

"May I use your phone?" she managed to choke out.

"Certainly," Mrs. West said. "Just dial nine. I'll be in the other room."

Hayley picked up the receiver. For a moment, she paused before raising it to her ear, half afraid of hearing either those disembodied voices or that awful screeching.

There was nothing but a dial tone.

"My fault, my fault," she muttered as her fingers made awkward attempts at dialing the Wilders' number.

Jamie answered the phone.

Hayley's mind worked at hyperspeed.

"Jamie, I—a friend said Taylor—"

She was shaking so hard she could hardly speak. Tears streamed down her face. Taylor was dead and it was all her fault.

"What about Taylor?"

Strangely, Jamie didn't sound upset. He sounded cheerful.

Hayley swallowed.

She forced herself to speak clearly.

"I heard that Taylor was ... sick."

"Sick?" Jamie sounded confused. "No, Taylor's fine."

"Where is she?"

"That's a strange question," Jamie said. "She's in her crib, napping."

"Check on her, will you?"

"Hayley, this is crazy . . ."

"Please, just check on her!"

After a moment of silence, she heard Jamie growl something about Hayley being as bad as Julianna.

Then he said, "Wait here."

Hayley stared up at the ceiling, out the window at the ocean, over at the white wicker couch, once more at the ocean. She didn't realize she was twisting the phone cord so hard her knuckles had gone bone-white.

Jamie returned.

"Taylor is just fine," Jamie said. "What the hell is this all about?"

The frantic tears that had spilled from Hayley's eyes flowed even more freely, and she choked back a sob. He hadn't gotten to Taylor after all.

"Hayley, my wife said someone tried to hurt the baby the other night," Jamie said.

Hayley choked on a sob.

"Wh—what?"

"I called the police," Jamie continued. "They didn't find anything, and I thought Julianna was dreaming. She walked into the wall so hard she broke her nose! Do you know anything about that, Hayley? 'Cause I'm having a hard time convincing Julianna it really *was* a dream."

A dream like Hayley's dreams. A dream like Kate's Shadow Man.

"I'm sorry," she blubbered. "It's just that so many things have been going wrong. I've had to cancel all future bookings because we've lost Kate and Hana. When I thought Taylor was sick, I thought . . . I thought . . ."

She fought back tears. The idea of that sweet little baby falling into Bruce's evil clutches was too much to bear.

"You thought someone came after Taylor, too," Jamie said evenly. "You don't have to worry about us, Hayley. Julianna's never going back to Jackal, no matter what. I don't know who's after you, but I'm not letting him get my family."

This time, Hayley's voice was strong and steady as she spoke.

"I don't blame you," she said. "I'm sorry for what's happened."

Jamie sighed. "Well, we're okay, after all. But I'm going to keep my eyes open. God help anyone who comes near my family!"

Hayley mumbled good-bye and hung up. Then, after a quick but polite farewell to Mrs. West, she left. She drove at once to Aidan's house, never taking her eyes from the road in front of her. She didn't want any more visions. She didn't want Bruce to have another chance to torment her.

She was unaware she was crying until she saw the concerned look on Aidan's face as he opened the door. He brought her inside, keeping an arm around her.

"What is it, Hayley?" he asked. "What's wrong?"

Lady jumped at her, but Aidan shooed away the puppy.

"Aidan, I think Bruce went after Julianna's baby," Hayley said as they sat down on his couch.

Resting her head on his shoulder, she explained the situation to him.

"It was a warning," Aidan said. "All those visions you saw along the road just mean he's getting stronger. We've got to do this séance, Hayley, and fast. Do you know if Kate's out of the hospital yet?"

"I haven't heard from her," Hayley said. "I'll give her a call. Can we all get together tonight?"

"It's okay with me," Aidan said. "If it's okay with Kate."

Kate agreed to attend, but Hayley could hear the doubt in her voice as they spoke on the phone.

"Do you even know what you're doing?" Kate asked.

Hayley thought of the visions of Jack and Kelly. She thought of that long-ago visit from her brother, Ricky.

"I've had some . . . experience . . . with ghosts."

When she hung up, she turned to Aidan.

"I've got to go home," she said. "I've got piano students this afternoon."

"Hayley, I don't think it's safe," Aidan said.

"Do you think it matters where I am?" Hayley asked angrily. "Bruce came all the way from Boston to get me. His spirit is connected to me wherever I go!"

Aidan stood up and took Lady's leash down from a hook on the wall.

"Then I'm coming with you."

"Fine," Hayley said. "You can veg out on the beach while I work."

She arrived home just in time for her first student. While Aidan did paperwork out on the deck, she taught. Still expecting something to happen, Hayley could barely hear the music. She told herself she didn't feel strange, yet she couldn't help her fearful anticipation. At one point, between students, Aidan asked if she was all right.

"I don't know," she said, rubbing her arms. She stood out on the deck, the ocean breeze ruffling her hair. "I don't think he's here now, but I'm afraid of when he'll show up."

"I'm here," Aidan reminded her.

Hayley smiled at him. They were kissing when the doorbell rang. She went inside to let in Nicky Cortez, her last student. The phone rang while the eleven-year-old plowed through "Blue Danube." Nicky hated piano, but his parents were insistent. They thought that knowing an instrument would help round-out the child who was only interested in baseball.

For some time Hayley had considered talking to them, telling them in a polite way that they were wasting their money. Nicky had been coming here for three years and hadn't enjoyed one moment of it.

Today she didn't even cringe when he hit a wrong note.

She picked up the phone.

"Hayley, it's Andy," the man said. "Something strange has happened."

Oh, not again!

"Did you read the paper yet?"

"I glanced at it," Hayley said. "Why?"

"Did you see the article about WDEM? It was a fair-sized headline."

Hayley saw the paper on the kitchen counter and started leafing through it.

"I'm looking right now," she said. "Why?"

"Do you remember that I used to work for WDEM?"

"Sure," she said, "But Andy, are you sure the article is in today's paper? There's nothing here about WDEM at all."

"Someone pulled a terrible prank, then," Andy said. "A sick joke. They went to a lot of trouble to have a newspaper made especially for me."

"Why?" Hayley asked.

"The article was about a fire that happened when I was working there," Andy said. "I knew something was wrong when I saw the paper, because WDEM has been closed down for years. Someone is just trying to torment me."

From the other room, the piano suddenly sounded ... different.

"I don't understand," Hayley said.

She heard Andy breathe. "I do. I was thinking about Wayne Boyer, and that poor little Japanese girl. The fire was ... a great calamity in my life. I think my newspaper was some kind of warning. Hayley, please be careful."

"I'm taking precautions until this man is found," Hayley assured Andy. He'd never believe her if she told him who was causing her problems. "I've canceled our bookings temporarily."

Hayley realized that Nicky was somehow playing better than ever before.

"You know," she said to Andy, trying to stay focused on the conversation, "I haven't had a chance to contact Sean about this. Would you mind?"

"Sure I'll do it," Andy offered. "The boy's going to need some words of encouragement. I'm sure he'll be disappointed."

"We all are," Hayley said.

"It's just a bunch of rotten luck," Andy said.

The "Blue Danube" rang through the house, loud and clear and ... perfect.

"But we'll be back," Hayley vowed.

"I know you will," Andy encouraged.

The "Blue Danube" segued into another song, a more modern one. After a few bars, Hayley recognized it.

"Andy, I've got a student here," she said. "I'll talk to you soon."

She barely heard Andy's good-bye as she hung up. She hurried into the living room.

"Nicky, who told you to play that song?"

Instantly, Nicky's fingers faltered. He hit a sour chord before turning to face her.

His face was guileless.

"It was behind the other music," he said. "You had a note clipped to it."

He handed it to her. Hayley felt her heart sink. The sheet music was "Tell Me That You Love Me." It had been her and Jack's favorite song.

"That's enough for today," Hayley said. "You can go now."

Nicky's brown eyes rounded.

"But . . . have I been here a whole half hour?"

She realized she'd cut him short by fifteen minutes. She forced a bright smile.

"Nicky, you played so well today," she said, "that I think you deserve a break. Why don't you go out and play on the beach until your Mom comes?"

"Wow!"

Nicky shot off as if the piano bench had become searingly hot. Hayley walked outside and sat on the edge of the deck, not daring to take her eyes from him.

"That wasn't much of a lesson," Aidan said, sitting down beside her.

"I had to cut it short," Hayley said. She handed Aidan the sheet music. "Bruce was here. This was our favorite song—Jack's and mine, I mean. Bruce left a note for Nicky to play it."

Aidan studied the note, written on paper decorated with small dolphins.

"Isn't that your handwriting?" he asked. "I recognize the swirling way you make *S*'s."

"It's my handwriting, all right," Hayley said, "but I didn't write it."

"Maybe you left it there and forgot about it?"

"I didn't," Hayley insisted. "I kept that songsheet in a box of mementos up in the attic. I haven't seen it since I packed it away, almost five years ago. Bruce is doing this to torment me."

Aidan thought for a few moments.

"You know," he said, "it could have been Jack. He could be sending you a message of encouragement."

Hayley looked up at him, surprised at his insight. Was it possible?

"Oh God, I hope so," she said. "I need all the encouragement I can get." She thinned her eyes a little. "Does it bother you that Jack might have sent me a message?"

"I think there's room enough for both of us," Aidan said, putting his arm around her. "For now, at least."

Hayley decided not to ask what he meant by 'for now.' Instead she settled against him comfortably and watched Nicky play with the dog. A short time later, when Nicky's mother showed up, Hayley lied about a severe headache to explain the short lesson. She returned the twelve dollar fee and promised to see Nicky next week. Nicky smiled at her, something he'd never done before.

"Thanks," he said. "I like the beach."

"See you next week," she said.

She turned back to Aidan, who was outside brushing sand from his legs.

"That's it," she said. "We're free now. What time is it?"

"Five-thirty," Aidan replied. "Dinnertime. Do you want me to pick up some Chinese?"

"Sounds great," Hayley said. "I'm going to take a jog along the beach while you're out. I've got a lot of tension to work off."

"I'm glad," Aidan said. "I was going to suggest you come with me. Just so long as you aren't alone in the house tonight."

Fifteen minutes later, Hayley stood in a jogging suit, watching Aidan drive away. Lady's head poked out the window, her ears flapping in the breeze. She looked so cute that Hayley couldn't help remembering the puppy she'd found.

She pushed the memory down. It would only upset her, and she didn't need that. Bruce did well enough on his own!

Hoping it would clear her mind, she set off at an easy pace. She noticed someone on the beach. He was lying on a red beach towel, propped up on his elbows, and seemed to be staring at her from behind dark sunglasses. Hayley, used to girl watchers, ignored him.

Until he took off the glasses.

It was Bruce Donner.

She gasped and slammed into something invisible.

"Lady, watch the line!" a teenager shouted.

She'd run into a fishing line, running from a pole stuck in the sand out to the water.

Hayley looked back at the man on the towel. It wasn't Bruce at all. It didn't even *look* like him.

"Get it together, Hayley," she told herself, running on.

She caught snatches of conversation.

". . . beautiful day . . ."

". . . can't we stay a little . . . ?"

". . . soda's warm . . ."

". . . be there that day . . ."

He was supposed to be there that day.

Hayley stopped and looked around. Many people were leaving the beach, but some were having picnic dinners. She half expected to see Jack and Kelly sitting on a blanket, waiting for her. But of course, that was just her nerves talking.

She felt a cramp in her side and stopped to work it away. As she was bending, she saw someone waving to her. It was Kelly, dressed in a pink bikini. Jack sat beside her on a blanket of his own. He patted the empty space beside him.

"We're waiting, Hayley!" Kelly called.

"Hurry," Jack said. "He's getting stronger again."

Hayley ran toward them, but she didn't seem to get any closer. The sand had grown strangely soft and wet. Like quicksand.

A huge crater opened up and swallowed Jack and Kelly in one gulp.

"No!" Hayley cried.

"It's okay, dear," someone said. "You just fainted."

"It's the running," another person said. "Some people do too much of this exercise business. They don't know when to quit."

Hayley blinked and found herself looking up at a circle of concerned faces. What had happened to her?

"You collapsed," an old woman said. "Do you want us to call someone?"

Hayley shook her head, forcing herself to her feet.

"I . . . I'm all right," she insisted. "What time is it?"

"Quarter to six," a man said.

"Are you sure you don't want help?" the old woman asked.

"No, no, I'll be okay," Hayley said. "I'm . . . I've got to go!"

She hurried away from the staring, befuddled group. Maybe it *had* been Bruce behind those dark glasses. Maybe he was watching her.

Maybe he knew of her plans.

19

When Hayley entered the house, Aidan was taking cartons of food out of a big bag. As he opened up a container of hot-and-sour soup, he seemed unaware of her disheveled state.

"Where do you keep the bowls?" he asked without looking up.

Unable to answer for the moment, still panting from her race back home, Hayley sucked in a deep breath.

"Aidan . . ."

"Hard run?" Aidan asked, looking up at last. The moment he saw her he hurried around the table to her side.

"Hayley, what happened?" he asked. "I'd say you look like you've just seen a ghost, but I'm afraid there's too much truth in it."

Hayley nodded quickly. "I did! Bruce was out on the beach, watching me. I went into some weird kind of trance when I was running, Aidan."

He put his arms around her and felt her trembling.

"Jack and Kelly appeared," Hayley told him. "They were trying to warn me, but the beach turned to quicksand and sucked them in. The next thing I knew, I was surrounded by people. They said I fainted, but I know I had a vision. Aidan, I'm sure Bruce is on to us. He knows what we plan to do tonight!"

"Then we'd better not waste any time," Aidan said. "Call Kate and tell her to get over here as soon as possible. In the meantime, I'm starving."

"I don't think I can eat," Hayley said. "I'm still shaking. It's one thing to have visions alone in my car, or in my bedroom. But on the beach in front of dozens of people? That was really scary."

Aidan said nothing. Instead he rummaged about the cabinets in search of dishes and utensils while Hayley made the call to Kate. When she hung up, she sat down at the table and discovered she was hungry after all.

"Kate's coming right over," she said. She took a spoonful of soup. "This is good. I'm surprised I can eat it."

"Survival instinct," Aidan said. "You're strengthening yourself for the night ahead."

"I wish food was all it would take," Hayley grumbled.

They had finished eating and cleaned up when Kate arrived. They went out to meet her in the driveway.

"I'm still not so sure about this," Kate said. "But you sounded desperate, Hayley."

Hayley gave her a hug. "You know I appreciate it." Thinking about the evening to come, she shuddered.

"Are you cold?" Aidan asked.

"Cold!" Kate cried. "It must be ninety degrees even now!"

Hayley led the way back into the house.

"I have a chill," she said. "It's just nerves. Does anyone want a drink?"

Aidan and Kate followed her inside.

"I could use a scotch," Kate said.

She knew where Hayley kept her liquor, and went to fix her own drink. Aidan opted for a Coke, while Hayley made hot cocoa. A few minutes later, they were seated around Hayley's kitchen table.

"So, how do we start?" Aidan asked.

"Don't you know?" Hayley replied. "This was your idea."

Aidan shrugged. "I don't know any other way to contact a spirit. I mean, I've seen movies where people sit around and hold hands."

"They usually have a medium," said Kate.

"If they're going to come at all," Hayley said, "they're going to come to me."

She finished her cocoa and took a deep breath. "All right, let's get on with this."

She got up and found a hurricane lamp to set in the middle of the table. While Aidan and Kate turned out the lights, she turned up the lamp's wick and lit it. Soon, they were bathed in yellow light that made their faces look more ghostly than any of Hayley's dream apparitions.

Hayley, Aidan, and Kate linked hands around the table.

"Who're we gonna call first?" Aidan asked quietly.

Kate giggled, thinking of the theme song from *Ghostbusters*. Hayley ignored her. She knew that Kate didn't take this seriously.

"Jack and Kelly," Hayley said. "We need their help. It's too dangerous to confront Bruce just yet."

Aidan breathed an audible sigh of relief.

"All right, let's go," Hayley said.

She closed her eyes.

"Jack? Kelly? Are you there? I need you. Please come to me now. Please . . ."

All the lights in the house went on.

"That was quick," Aidan whispered.

"How . . . ?" Kate couldn't form the question.

"Please, Jack and Kelly. Please help us! He's going to kill again, and—"

"Oh, *shit!*" Kate screamed. Aidan turned to follow the direction of her stare, and sucked in a quick breath. Hayley opened her eyes.

"Jack . . ." she said.

He was standing in the doorway to the living room. His face was pale and edged in blue, and there was a perfect black circle in the middle of his forehead.

"The gunshot wound," Kate whispered. "Oh my God . . . oh my God . . ."

"Jack, what should we do?" Hayley asked, unafraid.

"Be careful, Hayley," Jack said. "Be very careful. He's growing too strong."

"Hayley . . ."

They turned to the other voice and saw Kelly standing at the other side of the kitchen, holding the black balloons.

"Ask her what the balloons mean," Aidan whispered.

Hayley repeated Aidan's question.

Kelly, looking pretty despite her ghastly white skin and shattered temple, smiled.

"For the party, of course."

"The party?"

"The party!" Kate cried, excited by the revelation. "They mean the party you were going to have the day they died!"

Jack turned to her and smiled. "You are Kelly," he said. Then he nodded at Aidan. "You are me."

"I'm you?" Aidan asked, befuddled. "I don't understand."

"Use them, Hayley," Jack said. "Use their help. Kate is Kelly, Aidan is me."

Hayley hardly took in any of this. She was still thinking about the party.

"Jack, who was supposed to be at the party?"

"He . . ."

Suddenly, Jack's eyes went wide. He started making strange choking noises.

"Jack!"

The lights went out, came on again, and went out. Something fell over in the living room.

"He's . . . too strong!" Kelly wailed.

"Bruce? Is Bruce here?" Hayley asked, frantic.

"Hayley, get away!" Jack said.

Jack and Kelly vanished.

All the burners on the stove lit up simultaneously. The oven door popped open. Hayley looked inside to see Bruce's leering face. She screamed, and felt Aidan's hand tighten around hers.

The face disappeared.

Bruce was crouched on top of the refrigerator, laughing maniacally.

"I'm getting out of here!" Kate screamed, breaking the circle.

"Kate, don't!"

Kate stumbled away from the table, hit the door jamb, and maneuvered into the living room. The lights came on again. As Kate hurried for the door, pictures flew off the walls. The crystal figurines Jack had given Hayley shot across the room. With a cry, Hayley raced to save the little crystal mouse. She managed to catch it in mid-air.

She turned just in time to see another animal, an elephant nearly as big as her palm, hit Kate square on the temple. Kate hit the ground with a sickening *thunk*.

"Bruce, stop it!" Hayley screamed. "Please, stop!"

"No need to shout," said a calm voice.

Aidan came into the room, looking about for something that might come flying and knock him out, too.

"Oh, I'm not going to hurt you," Bruce said. He smiled. Bruce was sitting on the couch, legs crossed, one arm stretched across the back. "Not now. I'm not ready for you now. But I will be, soon."

With that, he disappeared.

For about half a second, Hayley could only stare at the spot where he'd been. The entire house was deathly quiet.

"I . . . never expected it to happen so quickly," Hayley breathed at last, staring at the disarray around her. She felt Aidan's arms go around her and turned to embrace him.

"Hayley, Hayley," Aidan whispered. "I thought . . . I didn't know what he was going to do. If he'd hurt you . . ." He hugged her all the tighter. "If I'd lost you, I don't know what I would have done. I love you."

The words seemed so warm, so good, among all this ruin, that for a moment Hayley could forget the horrors they'd experienced. She realized she loved Aidan, too. She'd been with him for weeks, but until this moment she hadn't admitted the strength of her feelings even to herself. It took the hatred of Bruce Donner to show her the love of Aidan McGilray.

"I love you, too, Aidan," she said. "So much."

They kissed briefly, then Hayley dropped to her knees beside Kate. Her friend was pale and still. "Oh, dear God, he's killed her!"

Aidan felt her wrist. "She's got a pulse. I'll get some water. See if you can revive her."

Hayley lifted her friend's head into her lap and patted her face. "Kate, wake up! Wake up!"

Kate's eyelids fluttered.

"My name is Kelly," she muttered.

Aidan came back with the water. Kate drank a little, then opened her eyes all the way.

"What's your name?" Hayley asked.

"What kind of question is that?"

"What's your name?" Hayley asked again, more firmly.

"Katherine Maria Reising," Kate said. She let Aidan help her to her feet. "Damn, my head hurts."

Hayley looked at Aidan.

"She said she was Kelly."

"That was what Jack said," Aidan reminded. "He said I was him, and Kate was Kelly. What do you suppose it means?"

Hayley breathed deeply. "I think I understand. Kelly was my best friend in Boston. Jack was my . . ."

She paused to look at Aidan, but the openness in his face invited complete honesty.

"I loved Jack," she said. "Jack wants the two of you to help me because you're in similar position to them."

She bent down to pick up a framed picture of her mother and father. As she hung the photo on the wall, Aidan and Kate started to help clean up. They hadn't come to terms with the evening's strange events so quickly, but sitting idly would have made them go crazy. They needed to do something, in all this quiet that might just herald more trouble.

"I'm worried it might be more than that," Hayley continued. "Maybe Bruce also sees you in the same roles as Jack and Kelly, and he hates you for it. You're closer to me than anyone else in Jackal, and it sickens me to think what he did to them."

"Oh ..."

Kate swayed, and Aidan caught her arm.

"Are you okay?" he asked. "Do you want me to take you to the emergency room?"

"I don't think any doctor could help me," Kate said. "I was just thinking about the Shadow Man."

She gazed at Hayley with imploring eyes.

"I don't want to deal with that again!"

"You won't have to," Hayley assured her. "I realized something tonight. Jack and Kelly haven't been able to speak clearly to me, and I think it's because Bruce is stopping them. But each time I've seen them, they've told me a little more. Tonight I got the biggest clue of all."

Aidan put a crystal giraffe on the shelf. Hayley adjusted it to the correct position.

"The party," he guessed.

"Exactly," Hayley said. "All along, Jack's been saying: 'You know who he is, he was supposed to be there that day.' What I need to do is find out who was going to attend the party. Somehow, one of those people is connected to all this."

Kate touched her head. There was a small bruise on her temple.

"You're confusing me," she said. "I thought that Bruce was doing all this."

Hayley couldn't help an ironic smile. "I guess you believe me now?"

"You bet I do!"

"Bruce *is* behind all this," Hayley said. "But he'd need a human counterpart for some things. Signing the paper for the dog, for instance, and canceling our show at Top-O'-the-Hill."

"Someone in Jackal Mystery Productions?" Aidan asked. "But who?"

"No one looks familiar to me," Hayley said. "The only men left are you, Sean, and Andy. If I'd known you in Boston, I would have recognized you by now."

"People change," Kate warned, eyeing Aidan suspiciously.

Aidan's eyebrows went up. "Don't stare at me like that. I'm not the one!"

"You've moved into Hayley's life pretty quickly, haven't you?"

"Yes," Aidan said, "because I found out right away that she's a wonderful person. I care for her—damn it, I love her. I'd never hurt her! And who's to say it's a man? People can wear disguises, change their voices. We're actors, for God's sake."

"Cut it out!" Hayley cried. "Don't let him make you enemies! I need you too much!"

Both Aidan and Kate breathed deep sighs, gave each other one last suspicious glare, and then turned to Hayley again.

"So, what do we do now?" Aidan asked.

"Ask questions," Hayley said. "Kate, you see what you can get out of Sean. Aidan, you take on Andy. I really don't think it's either one of them, but we have to be sure. I'm going to contact my old manager in Boston, to see if she can give me a list of names for the party. Maybe something will ring a bell."

By now the living room was completely cleaned up. They went around turning off lights, and soon the house was back in order, almost as if there had never been a confrontation. The dark circles under Hayley's eyes and the bruise on Kate's forehead, though, proved otherwise.

"Do you want to come back to my house tonight?" Aidan asked.

"All right," Hayley said without argument. She was

too exhausted to deal with anything more. "But I think Kate should come, too."

"Oh, no," Kate said. "I'd feel like a chaperone. I'll be okay at my place."

"I'm not sure that's safe," Aidan said.

Kate gave him a crooked smile. "Didn't know you cared."

Hayley started to speak, but Kate held up a hand. "Aren't you always insisting you won't be driven from your home?"

"But it's just for tonight," Hayley said.

"So, I'm safe tonight," Kate said, "but what about to-morrow night? He's going to come after me no matter where I am."

She laughed a little. "Besides, with the kind of rent I pay, there's no way I'm leaving my place until my lease is up!"

Seeing there was no arguing with her, Aidan nonethe-less insisted they'd follow her home. When they arrived at her apartment, all three went upstairs. At last Kate in-sisted she was fine and they should just leave. Hayley had a feeling she was right; she didn't sense anything strange in the place.

"I still don't like leaving her alone," she told Aidan as they drove to his house.

"He showed up when we were all together," Aidan pointed out. "Do you think it matters if she's alone or with us?"

"You make it sound hopeless," Hayley said.

Aidan turned to glance at her. She felt tears start, knew he could see them when, even as he faced the road again, he reached across the seat and took her hand, squeezing it. Without words, he told her it wasn't . . . couldn't be . . . hopeless.

20

Sean couldn't understand why Jackal Mystery Productions had closed down. Andy explained that it was only temporary, at least until they found out who was causing all the trouble. Besides, Andy told him, there weren't enough women in the cast now. Sean had been tempted to tell him he could dress in costume and take over one of the parts.

Hayley would probably think it was a terrific idea, and be grateful to him for saving the company. She was like a big sister, like someone he'd known for a long time. She'd be impressed by his clever idea, and wouldn't a man playing a woman's role make the show even funnier? It had been done before, with great success. He could do it. He was good at disguises.

He tried to call Hayley, but there was only static on her phone. The operator was of no help, claiming the line was out of order.

There was no point, he finally decided, in sitting around moping. He had to start looking for other work. His job at the service station didn't pay enough to keep up with Long Island rent, and he sure as hell didn't want to go back to Connecticut and live with his parents again.

He was poring over ads in *Variety*, hoping there might be a chance at something off-off-Broadway (better than silly dinner theater anyway) when the phone rang. He was surprised to hear Julianna on the other end of the line. He pictured her lithe, gorgeous dancer's body as he spoke to her. She, too, was upset about the sudden demise of Jackal Mystery Productions, and could he come over to talk? He said of course and promised to be there right after lunch.

When he arrived at Julianna's house, she was dressed only in a robe, with curlers in her hair. She squinted at him as if she didn't recognize him. The baby was suspended at her front in a sling, chubby legs dangling. He widened his eyes and tilted his head in a questioning manner, waiting for her to ask him in.

"What are you doing here, Sean?" she finally asked.

"You called me, remember?" he said, not understanding why she was acting so weird. "To talk about Jackal closing?"

"Oh . . ." was all she said as she stepped back. "I guess I . . . forgot. C'min."

She waved at the couch in the living room, then without a word left him alone. Sean took in the nice furniture, which was all coordinated peaches and greens but not one of those cheap matched sets. The lamps were brass and heavy-looking. Expensive. Jamie must make good money.

He realized he'd never been invited into her living room. They'd always gone straight down into the basement from the kitchen.

Julianna and Jamie didn't *seem* like snobs, and yet . . .

She was back, dressed in a multi-colored suit of parachute fabric, the curlers gone and her hair brushed. Taylor was on her hip now, and Julianna had a bottle in her other hand. She smiled at Sean as she sat down in a dark green wing-backed chair and began feeding the baby. Her demeanor had changed as much as her appearance.

"Isn't it strange?" she asked. "I'm so sorry this had to happen. Hayley seems like a nice person, don't you think?"

"I think she's great," Sean said. "I don't know why anyone would want to hurt her."

"Do you want a cold drink?"

Sean shook his head. "How's the baby?" he asked.

"She's fine," Julianna said. "Did you hear that someone tried to attack her the other night?"

Sean's jaw seemed ready to hit the floor.

"It's true," Julianna said. "The police and Jamie think I was dreaming, but I wasn't. I saw someone in her room."

Sean thought about the others who had been hurt. Everyone, it seemed, but Andy and him. Was he next?

"Maybe we ought to help Hayley," he said. "Maybe, if we brainstorm, we can learn the truth."

"Good idea," Julianna said. "I want to find the bastard who tried to hurt Taylor before he gets another chance!"

Sean gazed at a fruit basket on the coffee table, thinking. Silk fruit, inedible but delicious-looking. Like props. Like the knife that had hurt Kate.

"Do you still have the prop bag here?" he asked.

"It's in the basement," Julianna said. "Do you want to take a look at it? Do you think there might be a clue?"

Sean shrugged. "It's worth a try."

They went downstairs together, Julianna flipping on the lights from a switch inside the door. Still holding

Taylor, she pulled the prop bag from its place in one corner, then Sean picked it up and put it on the table. They pulled things out, hoping to find anything that might help solve the mystery. The table became strewn with funny noses, hats, a pair of oversized shoes, feather boas and more. Taylor, propped on the table in a baby seat, stared in fascination, her eyes glistened in the light from the hi-hats. Sean picked up a fake gun.

"I'm glad we were using a knife," he said. "The switch could have been made with this."

"Those realistic toy guns are illegal, I think," Julianna said. "I wonder where Andy got it from?"

"It's probably very old," Sean said. "He's been in show business for a million years, y'know."

He started to put the gun down, then turned to look into Julianna's blue eyes.

"You don't think . . . ?"

"He's the one with access to this sort of thing," Julianna said.

Sean considered this, then laughed. "He's such a nice old guy! Why would he want to hurt anyone, let alone Hayley?"

"I don't know, but . . ."

Suddenly, Julianna stopped and looked toward the stairs.

"I heard something," she said. "Hang on."

She went to the stairs and called up.

"Jamie?"

There was no answer. Julianna looked back over her shoulder.

"Stand by the baby, will you?"

She went upstairs and looked into the kitchen, calling Jamie once more. Then she came back down, shaking her head.

"I thought I heard Jamie come in," she said. "Sometimes he does his paperwork at home."

"Do you have a cat?"

"No," Julianna said.

"I do," Sean said. "She makes a lot of noise when she jumps on the counters."

Julianna made a face to say she thought cats jumping on counters was repulsive. Sean pulled a rubber chicken out of the box.

"Who had access to the back room at the restaurant the other night?" he asked, not really directing the question to Julianna.

"And who might have slipped poison into Aidan's coffee?"

Sean looked at her, impressed she'd made a connection there.

"Someone working at that restaurant," Sean said. "Maybe someone who tried out for Jackal but didn't get chosen?"

"How could he move from restaurant to restaurant?" Julianna asked.

"I don't . . ."

The screech of a smoke alarm cut him off. He looked at Julianna.

"Did you leave something on the stove?" he asked.

"No!" Julianna said, unhooking Taylor and picking her up.

There was a sudden rumbling noise, like a small explosion, from upstairs.

"Let's get out of here!"

Julianna started to run up the stairs, but Sean stopped her.

"Let me check the door first," he said quickly.

Sean's father, who had been a volunteer fireman many years earlier, had taught him safety rules. Following them now, Sean pressed his hand against the closed door, only to draw it back with a cry.

"It's burning hot!" he cried. "We can't go out that way—the fire must be in the kitchen! Damn, how could it spread so fast?"

"The windows!" Julianna said.

Working as quickly as he could, Sean pushed a table up to one of the three windows. He scrambled up and tried to open it, with no luck.

"It's painted shut," he said.

"Try the others!" Julianna wailed.

The baby had begun to cry, and Julianna rocked her back and forth, as Sean desperately tried to open the windows. They were all stuck.

"But that's impossible!" Julianna insisted. "Jamie had those open just a week ago! We were airing out the basement."

She began to cry.

"He's back again, and he's trying to kill my baby!"

Sean gave her a questioning look, but there was no time to ask what she meant. Smoke was seeping under the door from the kitchen. Sean looked around, spotted the laundry room door, and retrieved a towel from a basket of clothes. He ran upstairs again, shouting orders as he stuffed the towel around the bottom crack of the door.

"Get something to break a window!" he cried.

Julianna looked around and spotted a pair of dumbbells. She grabbed one and handed it to Sean as he ran down the stairs.

Within seconds, Sean was up on the table again, smashing at the window. Julianna pressed a hand against Taylor's head and turned away from the flying glass. She watched, shaking, as Sean gingerly yanked away shards that were still in the frame. When it was clear, he managed to squeeze himself through the opening. He could hear faroff sirens. The outside air was heavy with smoke, and from the corner of his eye he could see flames shooting out a window.

"Give me the baby!" he shouted, reaching into the basement.

"No!"

"Julianna, you can't climb up with her!"

"No, he'll cut her! He wants to kill her! He wants to kill her!"

In spite of his terror, there was room for surprise when Sean heard Hayley's voice behind him. He turned for only a moment, barely seeing Aidan at her side.

"Julianna called me," she said. "She said I should come right over."

Sean shook his head, then turned back to talk to Julianna. He knew she hadn't called Hayley, and realized she must not have called him, either. It was all a trick, a trap.

"Julianna, give me the baby!" he demanded.

"You'll cut her!" Julianna screamed.

"No!" Hayley said. "We've got to get her out of the house! Hurry, the fire's spreading!"

Seeing Hayley's familiar face had a calming effect on Julianna. Slowly, staring at her friend with tears in her eyes, she handed up the baby.

"Don't let him hurt her," she said.

"I won't," Hayley said, turning to run as far away from the fire as possible. Aidan kept at her side with a protective arm around her.

Neighbors were gathering to watch the spectacle.

The sirens grew louder, closer.

Sean reached into the window to help Julianna. Without Taylor, she didn't hesitate to grab him. She was halfway up to the window, her face very close to his, when he smiled at her.

And then he wasn't Sean at all. He was the same man who had tried to hurt Taylor the other night. Julianna screamed.

"I've got your baby now," the stranger breathed, in the same horrible way he'd spoken in the nursery.

Then he gave Julianna a hard shove, knocking her back off the table.

Sean turned and ran toward the police officer who had just emerged from his car.

"She fell off the table!" he cried. "She fell off when I tried to help . . ."

An explosion took out the side of the house. Aidan knocked Hayley and Taylor to the grass, covering them protectively. People began running and shouting. The police officer, alerted by Sean, told the firefighters there was a woman trapped in the basement.

More police arrived, ordering people far away from the scene. In the background, Hayley heard someone say it was a miracle no one was standing near that side of the house when it blew.

"Aidan, Julianna's still down there!" she cried over the din of sirens and shooting water and rumbling flames.

"They'll get her out!"

Firefighters in special suits worked their way into the house as others tried to put out the fire. Smoke billowed up into the sky. The air, already heated by the summer itself, was growing almost unbearable. Hayley, Aidan, Sean, and the baby moved farther away.

They watched as the firemen worked. Within ten minutes, the ones in spacesuits came out. One held something in his arms, hurrying toward a waiting ambulance.

"Oh, my God," Aidan said softly. "That's her."

"Is she dead?" Sean whispered.

"I don't know," Hayley said.

And yet, she did know. She knew that Bruce had taken another victim. Julianna Wilder was dead.

Suddenly, Taylor began to wail, as if she understood that her mother had been taken from her.

When she heard the baby, something snapped inside of Hayley. She pulled the baby tightly to her and looked up at the sky, a beautiful blue sky that only hid the darkness where evil spirits dwelled.

"It was Bruce!" she cried. "He did this! I know he did!"

"Hayley, people are . . ."

She didn't hear Aidan's warning. She went out into the middle of the street, still looking at the sky, still clutching Taylor.

"Where are you?" she screamed, "I want to see you, Bruce!"

People turned to stare at her. Aidan hurried to her side. Hayley shook him off, but he took her again in a firmer grip and brought her back to the lawn. Overcome by anger as much as by smoke and heat, she handed the baby to Aidan, then collapsed to her knees. She gazed through the hair that hung down over her watering eyes at the destruction Bruce had caused.

"I'm taking the baby over to that policewoman," Aidan said.

Hayley watched him, her hands grabbing clumps of grass, ripping it up. A few moments later, she saw Jamie exiting a car. She stood up slowly as he ran to the policewoman and took Taylor. The two spoke quietly. A stricken look came over Jamie's face, and the policewoman grabbed him around the shoulders to keep him from falling. Seeing that sorrow, brought on by Bruce's evil, made Hayley even more determined to put a stop to this. She looked up at the billowing column of smoke, fists clenched at her sides.

"Right here, right now!" she bellowed. "Let's *finish* this!"

A black and red light suddenly appeared in the middle of the street. Hayley knew by the way people ran about that everyone else was oblivious to it. She knew the light was Bruce, ugly and evil and hateful. But she was too in-furiated to be afraid of it. She took a step forward and heard his mocking laughter.

"Not yet, Hayley. Not yet. I'm not finished with the others."

Then the light was gone, as if sucked into another dimension. Hayley felt the pull of it, so strong it dragged her to her knees. She had to fight *that*.

21

Acting on an anonymous tip, the police questioned Andy Constantino as a suspect in the fire that had killed Julianna Wilder. Andy protested his innocence, but a computer check had revealed that he'd been responsible for the WDEM fire many years earlier. Fortunately, Andy had attended a Charlie Chaplin film festival at a nearby library with a group of friends. Plenty of witnesses could prove he was nowhere near the Wilder house at the time of the fire. As he left the precinct, Andy couldn't help wondering who had set him up. Was it the person who'd sent him the mysterious newspaper about WDEM?

He decided that Hayley deserved an explanation, and drove straight to her house. She greeted him at the door in shorts and a sleeveless shirt, barefoot. Her freshly washed hair dripped around her shoulders.

"Who's that?" he heard Aidan call from another room.

"Andy," Hayley said. She invited him in.

"I thought we should talk," Andy said.

"Me, too," said Hayley. "Have a seat, Andy."

Andy settled into a heavy wooden rocking chair. Hayley sat on the couch. Andy was nervous, wondering if she'd believe him, but the inquisitive expression on her face helped him relax just a little. She wanted to understand, not accuse him. She was open to explanation.

"Please believe me when I say I had *nothing* to do with that fire," he implored. "I really liked Julianna, and most of all, I'd never harm a child!"

"I know," Hayley said.

"I admit I started a fire at the radio station years ago," Andy said, "but it was an accident. I was drinking too much at the time and I blacked out . . ." Her response finally registered. He paused and looked in her eyes, trying to find sarcasm in her expression. Her face was still open and kind.

"You believe me?"

"I know who set the fire," Hayley said.

"Have you told the police?" Andy asked.

Aidan came into the room, his hair damp.

"It's going to take a lot more than the police to stop this guy," he said.

"Who is he?" Andy asked. "I want to know who set me up, who killed Julianna."

"His name is Bruce Donner," Hayley said. She'd looked at Aidan before she spoke, and Andy saw an unspoken agreement fly between them.

Andy looked down at his hands, thoughtful.

"Bruce Donner," he said, shaking his head. "It doesn't sound familiar."

"He was someone I knew when I worked in Boston," Hayley said. "He was in love with me and I didn't know it. I was going to marry another man, and Bruce couldn't take it."

"So he came all the way down here to persecute all of us?" Andy asked. "He must be crazy."

Hayley took a deep breath. "It's more than that. Andy, can I get you a cup of coffee? An iced tea? I've got a very long story to tell you."

While Andy was talking to Hayley and Aidan, Kate had a visitor of her own. Sean had stopped by, needing to talk to someone about the fire. He'd looked so forlorn, so desperate for company, that Kate had invited him in and given him a tall glass of iced tea. Sean drank it all down, then waited as Kate filled a second glass before speaking.

"Oh, my throat's so sore," he said. "The fire was unbelievable, Kate. I've never seen so much smoke."

"I spoke to Hayley on the phone," Kate said. "I hear you tried to save Julianna."

Sean lowered his head and closed his eyes, the glass suspended in his hands between his knees.

"She fell," he said. "I just couldn't help her. I tried, but I couldn't!"

It seemed he was going to start crying. Kate put a hand on his forearm.

"You did the best you could," she encouraged. "And you did save Taylor."

Sean opened his eyes and stared into his tea. He seemed to be studying a crystalline formation within the ice. Slowly he turned to look at Kate. Now there was no fear in his eyes, no remorse. Only a strange, almost reptilian coldness that made Kate let go of his arm and back away a little.

"The baby was supposed to be part of it."

It wasn't Sean's voice at all. It was deeper, full of evil, terrifying in its familiarity.

"Sean?"

She knew it wasn't Sean. Kate's knees seemed to turn cold and gelatinous, her bladder ached to let loose.

It was the Shadow Man.

No! No! No!

"You are not the Shadow Man," Kate said through clenched teeth. "There is no Shadow Man. You're . . ."

Not Sean. It was Sean she saw, but she knew the young man was gone. The voice, not just the Shadow Man . . .

The séance came back to her.

"Bruce?"

The man who looked like Sean but spoke like Bruce frowned.

"I'm not Bruce," another voice now, younger. It was more like Sean, but there was none of Sean's exuberance and openness in this man's expression. "My name is Roger Moran. And now I've got to kill you because you're *her* friend and she betrayed him."

Kate backed away as slowly as she could, afraid of upsetting him. Who the hell was Roger Moran?

Think of something to say! Talk to him, stall him!

Pray God talking would be enough to save her life.

"Roger?" she asked. "We . . . haven't met. Who are you?"

Sean sneered at her in disgust, as if she were too stupid to understand things.

"I worked with Hayley in Boston," he said. "Bruce was my idol, the man I looked up to . . ."

Suddenly, he closed his eyes. Kate started to stand up, but his hand shot out and grabbed her by the wrist. He squeezed tightly.

"You didn't die right the first time."

It was the Shadow Man's voice again. Kate struggled to pull away, grunting with the effort. Sweat began to pour down her temples; her heart was pounding. Dear God, how could he be so strong? Sean wasn't much bigger than she was!

"It was too quick and clean. This time I'll make sure you don't come back, Kelly!"

"Kelly?" Kate choked out, "I'm not . . ." Then she understood, recalling Jack's words: " 'Kate is Kelly.' Oh my God!"

She stopped struggling, angered and frustrated.

"Look at me!" she cried. "I'm *not* Kelly Palmer! My hair is brown, and she was taller, and prettier, and . . . and . . ."

Sean gave her wrist a jerk. "You're very pretty. Jack was good-looking, too. She always liked the handsome ones. She hated drunken slobs like me."

"You aren't a slob." *Try to appeal to his ego, try to show that you're on his side.* "Hayley just didn't understand. She didn't see how much she meant to you. But she liked you, Sean . . . I mean Bruce! She liked you a lot. She told me . . ."

"Don't patronize me!"

Still holding fast to her wrist, he swung his arm with unnatural strength, knocking Kate to the floor. Her mouth felt wet and thick. She touched it with a shaking hand and drew back blood-stained fingers.

"You're going to die for real this time," he said. "You, and then Jack. I know you're inside this woman, Kelly. I know Jack is inside that Aidan. It's the reason why Hayley likes him so much, isn't it?"

Kate only stared at him, too stunned to move or talk. Tears streamed down her face, mixing with the blood her teeth had cut from her lower lip.

He kicked her ribs.

"Isn't it?"

Kate gasped for breath, pain searing her chest. She

couldn't just lay here! If she didn't run, he would kill her for certain. She grabbed for the couch and started to pull herself up. It felt as if her body weighed a ton.

"I'll drive you away!" Sean screamed in Bruce's voice. "I'll drive you away and then I'll carve my words into Hayley's stomach and hang her up and we'll all be even."

He grabbed Kate, who screamed and struggled to pull away. Her mouth hurt, her chest burned, but she had to ignore these pains. She had to get away from him!

She screamed again.

"Somebody help!"

Somewhere in her mind, she wondered why the neighbors weren't coming. Somewhere else, she knew they couldn't hear her. Bruce was keeping the sounds within these walls.

"Hold still!"

But Kate would not hold still. There would be no one to help her. She was on her own.

Survival instinct kicked in with that realization. She screamed and fought with all her might, ignoring her pain, her fear. She pulled Sean along as she struggled toward the door. A step forward, a pull back. The apartment seemed huge.

His maniacal laughter filled the room. Kate spotted the small brass rocking horse she kept on the telephone table. She stopped struggling. The action threw him off-guard, but he still held her prisoner. Then she drew back her head and spat at him as hard as she could.

"You *bitch*!" Sean screamed.

He let her go.

Pain shot up Kate's side as she leaped toward the horse, her fingers extended as far as she could force them. Just a little more . . .

She grabbed the brass horse.

She turned and swung.

It went through nothing. Sean was no longer there. There was no one there.

No one but the Shadow Man.

The voice of the black figure was quiet and refined.

"For shame," he said. "Is this any way to treat an old acquaintance?"

Summoning all her courage, Kate raced for her bedroom. The Shadow Man was only a dream, she told herself. This was a nightmare, like the one she'd had the other night. She had to call Hayley, to warn her that Bruce was coming!

Kate locked the bedroom door and hurried to the phone by her bed. She dropped onto the bed to stop her knees knocking. Despite her shaking hands, she somehow managed to punch all the right buttons. She watched the door, knowing the lock was no protection from a ghost, but drawing comfort from it nonetheless.

Hayley answered.

"Hayley, it's Sean!" she cried.

On the other end of the line, she heard Hayley say, "Kate," but she just kept talking.

"The connection is Sean! He thinks he's Bruce Donner. I mean . . . I mean . . . he *is* Bruce Donner!"

Miles away, Hayley heard the sound of glass breaking; then Kate screamed. The line went dead.

Hayley hung up the phone, fear widening her eyes.

"He's got Kate," she said.

"Who?" Andy asked. "The man who set the fire?"

"Bruce Donner," Hayley said. "Aidan, we've got to get him away from her!"

Andy stood up, shaking his head. "I can't believe this. Ghosts! If Kate is in trouble, you should call the police."

"There isn't anything the police can do for her now,"

Aidan said. "Andy, we could use your help. I've got to warn you, it's going to be dangerous."

"I don't know . . ."

"No time to argue," Hayley said, setting the hurricane lamp in the center of the kitchen table. "Sit down and hold hands."

"A séance?" Andy asked with surprise.

Hayley did not reply. Andy's hand felt big and clammy in hers. Aidan's was warm, his grip very firm. She knew that he held on so tightly because he remembered how fast the spirits had shown up last time. And this time, it wasn't Jack and Kelly they were summoning. It was Bruce, in a desperate attempt to get him away from their friend.

She concentrated intently on Bruce, picturing him at Kate's apartment. Images of Kate backing away from him, screaming, formed in Hayley's mind. There was blood on Kate's mouth.

Hayley winced at a sudden pain under one arm.

"What's wrong?" Aidan asked.

"Pain . . . in my side," Hayley gasped. "He kicked her . . . in the ribs. I can feel it!"

"Sympathy pain," Andy said in amazement.

Hayley took a deep breath, then cried out on the exhale:

"Bruce! Bruce Donner!"

The air grew suddenly hot and thick. Andy began to wheeze. Aidan looked at him with concern, but the older man shook his head in reassurance and drew Aidan's attention to Hayley. Sweat was trickling down her face. Her eyes were closed, but the expression on her face told them she was seeing something terrible.

"Hayley?" Andy called softly.

She didn't hear him. Her mind had travelled to Kate's apartment. She felt like a ghost herself, standing at the sidelines, watching someone who appeared to be Sean lift Kate into the air with one powerful arm. It wasn't Sean at all, she knew. Bruce had taken over the young man's body. Hayley tried to call out, to move forward, but she was frozen to the spot. Bruce and Kate seemed completely unaware of her presence.

As Kate struggled, screaming and thrashing, Bruce carried her in a fireman's hold to the window. His free hand reached toward the pane. A blue light shot from his palm, blasting through the glass, shattering it into a million pieces.

Hayley shouted, *"Kate!"*

For a moment, her friend stopped struggling. She reached toward Hayley with a bloodied hand, her fingers outstretched.

"You've got to stop him, Hayley! Stop him!"

"I don't know how! Dear God, I don't know what to do!"

"What's he doing to her?" Aidan demanded, back in Hayley's house. "Hayley, what do you see?"

Somehow Hayley found the strength to speak, though her attention was claimed by events unfolding in Kate's apartment. "He . . . he's . . . Oh, dear Lord, he's hanging her out the window!"

At Kate's apartment, Hayley's mind-self lunged forward. In the beach house, she let go of the men and threw herself across the table, reaching, reaching . . .

"Bruce!"

"Bruce, let her go! You want me! I'm here!"

Hearing her at last, Bruce turned around. It was Sean Crane's face that wore the surprised expression. But it was Hayley whose screams filled both the apartment and the house.

He'd dropped Kate out the window.

"He killed her! He killed her!" Hayley sobbed into her

hands. Her vision of Kate's apartment had completely disappeared. Aidan took hold of her shoulders.

"What did you see, Hayley?"

"He dropped her! He killed her! He . . ."

A plant stand fell over, dirt and ceramic scattering across the floor. The door of the VCR opened and a tape shot across the room, smashing against the wall. The television went on full blast, the laugh track of an old sit-com filling the room like the voices of maniacal spirits.

"Bruce!" Hayley yelled, looking around the room.

Aidan cried out as his chair was jerked back from the table. All at once his face went completely white. His mouth dropped open as if to scream, but only a thin hiss of air came out.

"He's choking!" Andy cried, jumping up, desperate to help his friend. But what could he do? Aidan had not drunk or eaten anything that could be stuck in his throat. Pounding him on the back would probably be useless. Still, Andy had to try *something*. He moved toward Aidan, but something pulled him back and threw him across the room.

"No!" Hayley screamed. "Leave him alone!"

The temperature, already stifling, seemed to jump ten degrees. Andy crawled across the floor, gasping, reaching for the support of the coffee table. Pulling himself to a kneeling position, he watched in amazement as a bright red cloud, splotched with black, formed behind Aidan. The younger man was turning blue, his eyes half shut and streaming with tears. He was clawing at his neck, desperately trying to grab hold of something no one could see. Hayley was screaming, "Stop it! *Stop it!*"

The red cloud began to shimmer. Aidan fell from the chair, his urgent gasps filling the room. Hayley knelt beside him, holding his head in her hands but all the while staring at the red and black cloud. It started to swirl, becoming a vortex. The molecules that fabricated it began to coalesce, collapsing in on themselves into a more solid form—a man's figure.

Andy got slowly to his feet. He was shaking so badly he wasn't sure he could support his own weight.

"The Shadow Man," Hayley whispered, easing Aidan's head to the floor and standing up herself.

"What is that?" Andy asked in a tremulous voice.

No one answered. Aidan stared up at Hayley with a blank expression on his face. Andy wanted to make sure he was okay, but his shaking legs held him prisoner. He grabbed the side of the couch, afraid of collapsing. It was getting harder and harder to bear the heat in the room.

"Let me see you, Bruce," Hayley said. "The Shadow Man is Kate's fear, not mine!"

To Andy, she sounded more infuriated than frightened.

The man-shaped red shadow disappeared, instantly replaced by a man who looked as mortal as Andy or Aidan.

"Who the hell . . . ?" Andy said, startled.

The man turned and glared at him with bright red eyes that were fired with hate. Andy felt two spots of searing pain on his forehead, as if the eyes were projecting laser beams. He pressed a hand to his forehead and fell to the couch.

"Leave Andy alone," Hayley said, her voice strong. "He never did anything to you! Wayne, Hana, Julianna, Kate . . . what the hell did any of them ever do to you?"

"They were your friends," Bruce said.

"Oh, *bullshit*!" Hayley screamed. " 'If I can't have you, no one can,' is that it? Is that how you felt?"

"I loved you!"

"You never showed it!" Hayley shouted. "You never told me! I'm not a mind reader, Bruce!"

Sitting on the couch with his head in his hands, Andy heard hissing noises from different parts of the house and realized the water faucets had all gone on simultaneously. The washing machine had started, also. Hayley seemed oblivious to all the noise.

"You all *laughed* at me," Bruce growled. "You called me a has-been and a drunk!"

"I never did!" Hayley insisted.

"I saw you talking to those critics, the night of the thousandth performance," Bruce said. "I saw you laughing—you agreed with them!"

Andy recoiled as the coffee table split in half. A few feet away, Aidan had risen to his feet. He didn't seem at all disturbed by what was happening, and there was a strange look in his eyes. As Andy watched, Aidan's body jerked once, twice. He began blinking rapidly.

Afraid of what might happen next, Andy crept off the couch and backed slowly toward the door. Maybe he could get out while no one was looking . . .

"Oh, Bruce," Hayley said, her voice weary. "I never said a bad thing about you. You were my mentor, my friend. I cared very deeply about you."

Andy reached for the front door knob.

"No!" Bruce cried, pointing at him.

The knob jumped loose just before Andy touched it, flying up toward his face. It hit him square in the middle of the forehead. Andy stumbled, turning to look at Hayley with unfocused eyes before he fell over.

"Oh God," Hayley moaned. "Why don't you just go away and leave us alone?"

"I want you with me!" Bruce insisted. "And I want them to pay for keeping you from me."

"No one *kept* me from you!" Hayley cried. "I didn't love you! I loved Jack! You were my friend, Bruce. Just my friend. Get that into your head and get the *hell* out of my life!"

"Hayley . . ." Bruce's anger had begun to change. There was despair in his voice.

"Get away from me! I hate you! I *hate* you!"

Hayley was screaming in rage now, rage that had been building for the past weeks, perhaps for the past five years. How *dare* he do this to her? How dare he take away the two people who meant the most to her, and then come back to hurt her new friends.

"I *hate* you!" she screamed once more.

Bruce let out an ear-shattering moan. The television screen blew out; an iced tea glass left on an end table shattered.

Suddenly Bruce vanished, and the temperature of the room dropped back to normal so quickly that it seemed the heat was sucked into another dimension. Everything was quiet. A cool breeze blew around the room, ruffling the curtains and tossing Hayley's bangs into her eyes. She brushed them back.

"Aidan," she whispered, a choke in her voice. "Aidan, we've got to help Andy before he comes back."

Aidan didn't answer. He just turned slowly and looked at her with eyes that were not his own dark ones. His eyes were blue.

Jack's eyes.

anything that hadn't already been thrown to the floor. Hayley turned her head away, feeling it sting her arms.

"Jack, Jack, please end this!" she begged.

The wind stopped. Hayley turned back just in time to see Jack leap for Bruce. On impact, the two became swirling columns of light, one bright blue, one mottled red and black. Hayley covered her ears against the shrieks, squinted against the brilliance of the lights.

The ghostly tornado struck the sliding doors, shattering them into a million pieces. Each shard reflected shimmering light, some blue, some red, some black. The whole room was ablaze with reflections.

"Aidan!" Hayley screamed. Was he lost in the midst of the battle?"

Suddenly she felt a gentle touch on her arm. Andy must have come to.

"Andy . . ."

But it was Kate she saw when she turned. Kate was alive! Overcome with relief, Hayley moved to throw her arms around her friend. Kate stepped back quickly.

"No, don't touch me!" she said.

"Oh God, Kate, they're killing each other," Hayley said, reaching for her friend, but again Kate jerked away.

"Kate, what's wrong?" Hayley demanded. Behind her, the whirlwinds of light spun together in the center of the room, twining and shaking about each other. Their angry noise filled the air.

Suddenly, Hayley knew exactly why she couldn't touch Kate, knew how her friend had suddenly appeared in her home despite the ruined front door, despite what Hayley had seen in her vision.

Kate was no longer human. Hayley's vision had been true. Bruce had killed Hayley's closest friend. In despair, Hayley began to weep.

"I'm all right," Kate insisted. "I'm all right over here. But we've got to stop Bruce!"

"How?"

Hayley looked at the twist of lights, which had shifted to a corner of the dining room.

"The spirits have always crossed toward *you*," Kate said. "You drew them to this side. You did it with Ricky, with Jack ..."

"I didn't do anything! They just came to me." Hayley didn't understand.

Kate shook her head, frustrated. "You're strong, Hayley. Stronger than Bruce! All you have to do is pull him completely to this side. Aidan ... Jack ... will be stronger then. Just call to Aidan! Call him, Hayley! Bruce will follow Aidan."

"We'll both help you, Hayley," said a second, very familiar voice.

Kelly appeared beside Hayley, white light glowing around her. Hayley's two best friends flanked her, both torn from life by the same man. Now Bruce wanted to take away the man she loved, the way he'd taken Jack. She thought of all the people Bruce had killed or injured: Kate and Kelly, of Julianna, Wayne, and Hana. Most of all, she thought of Aidan, whom she loved now more than anyone in the world.

"*Aidan!*" Her scream was long and furious and powerful. It seemed to pull her spirit out of her body— suddenly she was surrounded by banners of blue, red, and black light. Though her feet were not touching the floor, she didn't feel as if she were floating or falling. Before her, she could see Jack and Bruce struggling in a desperate battle. There was no sign of Aidan. Kelly and Kate were still beside her. They seemed to radiate a peculiar warmth.

Bruce seized Jack by the throat, squeezing hard with

both hands. Jack brought the heel of his hand sharply up to Bruce's chin, but only managed to knock his head back a little. Bruce's iron-clad grip grew tighter.

Hayley watched in horror as Jack began to flicker. One moment, she could see right through him; the next moment he was solid again. When he faded out a second time, Hayley saw Aidan in his place. Jack had been drawing extra strength from Aidan, a living person. If Jack was forced into another dimension, he might take Aidan with him. She'd lose both of them.

"Aidan! Aidan, take my hand!" Hayley stretched toward him.

Aidan reached for her, but no matter how they struggled they couldn't make contact. Aidan turned his attention back to Bruce, twisting in his grasp.

"Bring him back to your side!" Kelly urged, wrapping a warm hand around Hayley's upper arm. Hayley felt new strength seeping into her.

"You can do it, Hayley! You've always been able to do it!" Kate said, duplicating Kelly's gesture.

Strengthened by her love for Aidan, and by the power now streaming into her from her two dearest friends, Hayley threw herself at Bruce with a cry of anger . . .

. . . and slammed right into the wall of the living room in her house, clutching Aidan's wrist in both hands. He wrenched away from her, shouting, "Get out! Get away while you can!" He launched himself at Bruce, who glared at them from the middle of the room.

"I won't leave you, Aidan! I love you!"

"I love you, too, Hayley!"

"Shut up!" Bruce roared. "She's mine!" He held up one hand and froze Aidan in his tracks.

Shackles appeared out of nowhere, slamming around Hayley's wrists and locking her to the wall. She looked from one wrist to the other in disbelief, then searched the room for her allies. Kate and Kelly had vanished.

"Watch him go to Hell," Bruce sneered.

Hayley screamed in futile protest, pulling at her shackles.

Bruce raised both hands, palms toward the other man. Aidan's eyes changed to blue; his face distorted until it became Jack's face. Then it flickered back to Aidan's, then to Jack's, as if the spirit was fighting to stay secure within the man's corporeal form. The effort seemed to be weakening both of them, because neither struggled to reach Bruce.

"Oh God, Jack, don't let him kill Aidan!" Hayley begged. There was no time to think. Bruce's hands began to glow with that strange black-and-red light. The evil light moved toward Jack, who seemed unable to move.

"Jack get away from him!"

Jack gazed at her in sorrow.

"Hayley ... Hayley, I'm sorry ... he's too ..."

Suddenly two brilliant white lights formed around Bruce. He spun in a circle, arms thrashing. He looked like a badly-controlled marionette.

Jack's relief—and renewed resolve—were obvious as he dissolved into a column of blue light and sped into the fray. The blue and white lights twirled together, braiding around Bruce's spirit, trapping it. It turned back into red and black light. Bruce's screams were so horrible that Hayley thought she would die. She clapped her hands over her ears, realizing as she did that the shackles had disappeared. She watched in wonder as the black and red in the center of the column grew more and more black, until it was nothing more than a shadow. Then even the shadow was gone.

The blue and white lights separated, and Jack, Kelly, and Kate stood before her.

"You're safe," Kelly said, smiling.

"Bruce won't ever come back again," Kate reassured her with a characteristic grin. Even in spirit, Kate knew the feeling of accomplishment.

Jack's gaze was warm and loving. "Remember that I loved you," he said.

"Jack, please." Hayley hurried toward him, but it was Aidan she caught in her arms as he collapsed.

"What the hell happened?" Aidan moaned.

Hayley looked at him. "You saved my life."

She kissed him, and imagined she was kissing Jack, too. Kissing him good-bye.

"You all saved my life."

23

Roger Moran, a.k.a. Sean Crane, pulled himself slowly to his feet and tried to make sense of his surroundings. He was in an apartment he didn't recognize, and yet he had a strange feeling he had come here on his own. He took in the knocked-over table and the shattered window. A photograph on a nearby shelf caught his eye. He picked it up—a pair of women.

He knew them, but in a way that someone knows a face from an old yearbook. He'd been talking to the one with light-brown hair a while ago . . .

Slowly, it came back to him. He'd been holding her—Kate Reising—by the ankles, hanging her outside the window. Startled, Sean ran to the window and looked down. The bushes two stories below were crushed, but there was no sign of Kate.

"What the hell have I done?" he asked himself, running a shaking hand through his hair. "What the hell have I done?"

He felt his pocket, found car keys, and hurried out of the apartment. Maybe she'd been taken away by an ambulance? But no one had come upstairs to check her apartment. There was still a chance he wouldn't be caught if he ran away.

Away from what? he asked himself. As he approached his car, a vehicle he somehow recognized despite his bewildered state, he realized there were huge holes in his memory. He clearly recalled his last day in Boston, vaguely remembered getting on the plane . . .

He flipped on the radio, his hand shaking.

"Hope you're enjoying the beach on this gorgeous August day," the announcer said cheerily.

August! He'd come to New York at the end of June.

"Oh God," he said.

He'd never had a blackout like this before. When he'd left Boston, he'd sworn to leave behind the world of drugs and booze that had swallowed him for a time: He was going to start fresh here, make a new life for himself. Somehow, though, he'd gotten messed up again. And he'd lost over a month of his life!

Hayley Seagel.

The name popped into his head. She would explain what had happened. She would help him understand. She . . .

Roger was so full of thought that he nearly ran a red light. He slammed on his brakes just in time. His heart pounded with excitement. He'd known Hayley Seagel five years ago, when he'd worked in her Boston theater company. After all that sorry business with Bruce Donner, he'd tried to get other acting work, with no success. The feeling of failure had pushed him into the world of addiction.

"God, Hayley, I hope I can find you," he said, "and I hope you can answer some questions for me."

He didn't need to ask the mundane question that every amnesiac seems to ask: "Who am I?" He knew who he was. What he wanted to know was, who had he *been*?

While Aidan tended to Andy, who had also reappeared the moment that Bruce vanished, Hayley kept herself busy, turning chairs upright and sweeping away shards of glass. She knew she was just postponing the inevitable. At some point, she would have to check on Kate. But as long as she stalled, she could pretend her friend was still alive. She could pretend it had all been a horrible nightmare, and that Kate would ring the doorbell at any moment.

Then the bell *did* ring.

"Do you want me to answer it?" Aidan asked quietly. They were all still shocked by what had happened.

"I'll do it," Hayley said, hurrying to pull it open, hoping beyond hope that Kate would be standing there.

It was Sean Crane. His hair was a mess, his clothes were disheveled and bloodied . . .

"Sean," Hayley said simply, recalling Kate's last phone call.

"My . . . my name is Roger Moran," Sean stammered.

Hayley gasped. "Roger? I don't understand. Why did you lie about your identity?"

Roger looked completely bewildered and frightened. There were tears in his eyes.

"I . . . I think I've done some terrible things," he said. "I don't remember any of the last several weeks."

"Donner must have been using him," Aidan said, coming up beside Hayley.

Roger regarded him blankly, then looked at Hayley

again. There was pleading in his eyes, as if he wanted to understand the nightmare he'd woken into.

"Come inside," Hayley said. She uprighted a wicker chair and put a cushion into it.

"Thank you," Roger whispered, sitting.

Now that she looked closely at him, she saw Sean's resemblance to Roger Moran, an actor she'd worked with in Boston. Roger had been at least sixty pounds overweight. His hair had been dirty blond hair, and he'd worn glasses. But she realized now that his eyes were the same. You can lose weight and color your hair, but you can't change the shape of your eyes.

She knew that he'd killed Kate, but she couldn't hate him. Though it had been his body, his hands, that performed the crime, Bruce had actually committed it. Sean—she still thought of him as Sean—had been used. He was a victim, too.

"Terrible things *have* happened," she said, "but we don't blame you for any of it. Listen to me carefully. As God is our witness, what I'm about to say is the truth."

When she finished talking, the look on Roger's face told her he believed every word she'd said.

"I feel . . . as if I've been somewhere else all this time, doing something I can't remember." He leaned forward and covered his face with his hands. "Oh God," he moaned. "I killed two people!"

"Sean, you didn't," Hayley insisted.

"My name is Roger," he corrected softly.

"Roger, of course," Hayley said. "Do you really think I could sit here and talk to you if I thought you were guilty? Bruce Donner *used* you."

"In a way, you're also a victim," Aidan said, putting a comforting hand on the man's shoulder. "Why don't you tell us what you remember?"

Roger nodded. He spoke quietly. "After . . . after those

things happened with Bruce," he said, "I became very depressed. I drank, took drugs, anything to avoid dealing with the murders, Bruce's suicide."

He looked at Hayley.

"I don't know how you coped so well," he said.

Hayley shrugged. "It wasn't easy for any of us," she said simply. She didn't want to talk about her own feelings.

"Finally I went for counseling," Sean continued. "When I finally came to terms with the facts, I decided I had to do something with my life. I hadn't been all that serious about theater, but now I knew how much I wanted to be an actor. I worked hard to lose weight, then colored my hair to go with my new image. I worked in theater in Boston for a while, then decided it was time to come to New York. I didn't even know you lived here, Hayley."

"Bruce probably took over before you got here," Hayley guessed.

"I remember the last time I saw him," Roger said. "It was the morning of the party Jack and Kelly were throwing for your anniversary."

"Oh!" Hayley said, sitting up straighter. She looked at Aidan. "Now I understand what Jack was trying to tell me. He kept saying, 'You know who he is, he was supposed to be there that day.' *Roger* was supposed to be at that party. Jack was trying to make me see that Bruce was using someone who was very close to me."

"The police," Roger said suddenly, his eyes wide with fright.

"The police think Wayne Boyer died from a snake bite," Hayley said. "And Julianna Wilder, God rest her soul, was killed in a freak fire. There's a cop who's somewhat suspicious about all the things that had happened to Jackal Mystery Productions. But if nothing more happens, she'll probably attribute it all to a stalker who decided to give up."

Andy moaned a little and tried to sit up straighter.

"Don't say a word," he offered.

"That's right," Aidan agreed. "You aren't guilty, and you shouldn't have to pay for crimes someone else committed."

"I still *feel* guilty," Roger said.

"That's understandable," Hayley told him. "But if *I* can sit here and tell you you aren't, considering I lost my best friend, then you aren't!"

Roger thought for a long time. No one spoke, letting him try to accustom himself to all this incredible information. At last he said:

"It's going to take some time to get used to all this."

"We'll help you in any way we can," Hayley offered.

Roger managed a smile.

"You always were kindhearted," he said. "I think that's why Bruce liked you so much. I'm glad to be working with you again, Hayley. I hope you'll keep me on—you were always a great director."

"Encouraging words," Andy said.

Hayley nodded with a smile. She needed all the encouragement she could get, because in spite of everything she intended to get Jackal Mystery Productions up and running again.

She said, "I think we'd better swear to each other that what we talked about here today, and everything that's happened, stays between us, a secret."

"I certainly don't want to face the police," Roger said. "I know that I killed those people—don't protest, it happened—but I also know I wasn't responsible. I can feel that, as much as I feel the guilt. But the police would never understand. And, God . . ."

His voice broke, but he closed his eyes to keep from crying again. "God, I don't want to go to jail!"

"You won't," Aidan insisted, holding out his hand. "I promise to keep the secret."

"So do I," Andy said, resting his hand on top of Aidan's.

Hayley followed. Finally, slowly, Roger put his own hand out. The pact was made; the secret would be kept . . . forever.

Epilogue

The dragon had returned to Hana Musashi's dreams.

Once it had been established that her injuries were not life-threatening, her uncle Leo had had her moved to a room in the north wing of his mansion. Leo, Mariko, and Yoshi took turns at round-the-clock vigil at her bedside, relieved only now and then by a nurse or doctor. They watched and worried as Hana slept fitfully. It was encouraging to see her respond to basic commands, to watch her jerk her foot back if prodded. But none of them could understand the pained expression on her face, one that appeared only when she was in a deep dream state.

"She's remembering the accident," Yoshi said, not knowing that Hana was seeing something far worse than that nightmare.

Through the hideous blood-rain, the dragon with mottled black-and-red scales swooped down at her from blazing clouds.

This night, the dream was different.

Hana was not alone.

Hayley stood with her, and Kate, and Aidan. Andy Constantino was with them. Sean Crane stood far away, as if afraid to approach. He kept watching the sky overhead.

Hana also saw two other people, a man and a woman she didn't recognize, but she knew that they, too, were there to help her rid herself of the dragon.

This time when it came flapping down from the golden sky, Hana looked straight at it. She didn't feel afraid of it now, not with so many friends to help her. Instead of cowering, she held her hands up, as if to welcome it.

Someone in the dream cried out, but Hana refused to budge. The dragon soared down . . .

. . . and became an eagle, talons curled and deadly.

"Give her life back to her!" cried the unknown man.

The eagle became a raven.

Then a crow.

Then a sparrow.

It was only a butterfly when it lit on Hana's outstretched arm. It flapped its wings once, then vanished.

Hana turned to thank her friends. They were all gone. There was only a blurry figure, speaking in soft tones.

"Hana-San?"

Hana blinked and saw her Aunt Mariko bending over her. Her brother and uncle stood there, too, concern in their eyes.

"He's gone," Hana whispered. "The dragon is gone." She closed her eyes and smiled, feeling at peace.

It was nearly three A.M. before Hayley and the men finished cleaning up. Hayley had phoned an anonymous tip into the police, telling them where to look for Kate's body. Andy insisted on going home, wanting to be in his own bed. Hayley and Aidan dragged themselves off to the bedroom, while Sean took the couch.

Hayley went to bed knowing the house was 'empty,' yet the memory of the night's horror was so strong that she clung tightly to Aidan as she fell asleep. She thought of the moment when he'd told her he loved her, and it helped her relax a little and feel safe.

She dreamed of Jack and Kelly.

"It's over," she told them.

"I love you, Hayley," Jack said. *"He loves you. Find peace with him."*

The balloons Kelly held were no longer black. Instead, they were bright and colorful . . . and whole. Jack handed Hayley a red baloon, smiling.

"Let him love you for me," he said.

Kelly released all her balloons. They floated up, toward a bright, beautiful light. When it disappeared, Jack and Kelly were gone, too.

Hayley woke up, feeling more content than she had in years. Tomorrow she would mourn her friend, but for now, she was calm. Quietly, she got out of bed and tiptoed into the living room. Sean was no more than a shadowy lump on the couch. The room was dark, except for a ray of moonlight that shone between the sheets they had nailed up to replace the broken glass doors. Like a beacon, it landed directly on the shelf of glass animals. Hayley picked up the crystal mouse and caressed it for a few moments. She knew she didn't really feel Jack's spirit within it, but she could pretend.

After a few moments, she kissed the mouse gently and put it back. She knew she wouldn't take it down again.

She needed it no longer.

THE BEST IN MYSTERY

ADVENTURES IN
ROMANCE FROM TOR

☐ 52264-8 AMBERLEIGH $4.99
Carole Nelson Douglas Canada $5.99

☐ 52266-4 FAIR WIND, FIERY STAR $4.99
Carole Nelson Douglas Canada $5.99

☐ 52160-0 JEWEL OF THE SEA $4.99
Susan Wiggs Canada $5.99

☐ 52265-6 LADY ROGUE $4.99
Carole Nelson Douglas Canada $5.99

☐ 51681-8 OCTOBER WIND $4.99
Susan Wiggs Canada $5.99

☐ 51930-2 THE RIVER'S DAUGHTER $4.99
Vella Munn Canada $5.99

☐ 58307-8 THIS WIDOWED LAND $4.99
Kathleen O'Neal Gear (March 1984) Canada $5.99

SUSPENSE FROM
ELIZABETH PETERS

☐ 50752-5   BORROWER OF THE NIGHT $3.95
Canada $4.95

☐ 51241-3   THE CAMELOT CAPER $4.50
Canada $5.50

☐ 50914-5   THE COPENHAGEN CONNECTION $4.50
Canada $5.50

☐ 50756-8   THE DEAD SEA CIPHER $3.95
Canada $4.95

☐ 50789-4   DEVIL-MAY-CARE $4.50
Canada $5.50

☐ 51908-6   DIE FOR LOVE $3.99
Canada $4.99

☐ 50002-4   JACKAL'S HEAD $3.95
Canada $4.95

☐ 50750-9   LEGEND IN GREEN VELVET $3.95
Canada $4.95

Buy them at your local bookstore or use this handy coupon:
Clip and mail this page with your order.

Publishers Book and Audio Mailing Service
P.O. Box 120159, Staten Island, NY 10312-0004

Please send me the book(s) I have checked above. I am enclosing $ _____
(Please add $1.50 for the first book, and $.50 for each additional book to cover postage and
handling. Send check or money order only— no CODs.)

Name _____

Address _____

City _____ State / Zip _____

Please allow six weeks for delivery. Prices subject to change without notice.